GHOST

Brooke MacKenzie

GHOST GAMES

GRAVESTONE PRESS

Table of Contents

GHOST GAMES

Dedication

*For Chase
a kindred spirit*

GHOST GAMES

The Elevator Game

It all started with something I saw on the Internet.

"Alice, you need to see this." My friend Kerry had been hunched intently over her laptop for the last half hour. I had been occupying myself with a particularly tricky crossword puzzle. In other words, it was a typical Friday night. We were not exactly prom queens.

She passed her laptop to me, and I watched security camera footage of what appeared to be a young woman having a nervous breakdown in a malfunctioning elevator. She enters the elevator wearing a red raincoat, pushes many buttons, and the doors remain open. She hides, and her mouth appears pixelated on camera. Eventually, she steps into the hallway and appears to be having a conversation with someone who isn't there. She leaves the frame and the doors finally close.

"Hmmm." I shut Kerry's laptop. "What's so interesting? A crazy chick in an elevator? I like your cat videos better."

"Wait, you didn't hear about this?"

"About a crazy chick in an elevator? Uh, no. Mr. Mentz's biology final has been my sole focus lately."

She sat next to me and put a hand on my shoulder, which meant I should pay attention, even though I had just figured out the solution to 13 down. Kerry told me the story of the woman in the red raincoat, who had traveled to California and was staying in The Cecil Hotel. I raised my eyebrows to let her know she had my full attention. Hearing the name of the hotel struck a major chord of recognition, just like Kerry knew it would.

The Cecil Hotel was located in Los Angeles's notorious Skid Row, and to say it had a checkered history is an understatement. It was, for instance, a final drinking spot of Elizabeth Short, who is better known as The Black Dahlia, perhaps the world's most famous murder victim. The Black Dahlia was found drained of blood, cleaned, and severed in half with a macabre grin slashed across her face.

In the 1960s The Cecil was nicknamed "The Suicide" for the amount of desperate and depressed guests who checked in, only to check out of their own lives. Richard Ramirez, The Night Stalker, nestled into The Cecil during his killing spree— even brazenly dumping his bloody clothes into the dumpster outside and casually strolling, half-naked, through the lobby and up to his room. The Cecil was, according to many paranormal enthusiasts, crawling with ghosts. Because of its grisly history and numerous reported hauntings, The Cecil was a favorite topic of mine. How could so much darkness exist in one place? Especially a place that seemed as innocuous as a hotel, with its room service and bell boys?

And so, the death of the young woman in the elevator, with all of its bizarre circumstances, could have only happened at The Cecil. She had been reported missing for several weeks when guests began complaining of poor water pressure, and the drinking water was brown and foul-tasting. When a maintenance worker dragged a ladder to the roof, took the treacherous climb to the water tank, and removed the heavy lid, he made a grisly discovery: the missing woman's body was floating naked, along with her clothing and personal effects nearby. The last time she had been seen alive was in the elevator video.

Kerry paused dramatically, letting the story settle in.

I went ahead and stated the obvious: "So, you're surprised that a woman who was clearly having some kind of a psychotic episode committed suicide?"

"Wait, just listen. By all accounts, this woman was the picture of mental health. Suicide just didn't seem to make any sense to anyone who knew her. And besides, if she had committed suicide that would mean that she had somehow gotten onto the roof without triggering the security alarm, managed to climb up to the tower without a ladder, and replaced the heavy lid from inside the tank.

"Her autopsy showed no sign of rape or trauma. She had no drugs in her system. Her death was ultimately marked 'undetermined.' No one really knows what happened to her."

Kerry's left eyebrow was raised slightly. I knew she had a thought brewing and was just waiting for me to ask the right question.

"Do you have a theory about what happened?"

She leaned even closer. "Have you ever heard of the elevator game?"

The elevator game is a Korean Internet legend. Put simply, it proposes that by pressing the right combination of buttons an elevator passenger can be transported to another dimension. The player finds an elevator that will preferably remain empty throughout the game in a building with at least ten floors. The player enters the elevator on the first floor and then visits the fourth floor, allowing the doors to open without getting off. Then, the player presses the button for the second floor. Then the sixth. Then back to the second. Usually, at this point in the game, a woman enters the elevator, and one of the game's most important rules is invoked: do not interact with the woman. Do not look at her. Do not speak to her. She will try to get your attention, but if you interact with her, she will lure you to the other dimension and you will be stuck there forever. The player must go back to the second floor, and then up to the tenth. The doors will open and the player will see that the hallway is plunged into darkness. While the hallway may look identical to the one in the building, at this point, the player is actually in another world entirely. Entities may appear that will try to confuse the player and lure her out of the elevator. Once out of the elevator, it can be very difficult to find a way back. If the darkness is not enough of a clue that the player is in another dimension, there will also be a red cross glowing in the background, like an eerie welcome sign. No matter what, the player must somehow make her way to the fifth floor and then back to the first for the game to finally end.

"Are you saying that you think the elevator

game had something to do with this mysterious water tank death?"

"Absolutely. I believe, as do many others from what I've read on Internet forums, that what we were seeing on that video was not a woman having a breakdown. We were seeing the elevator game. She wasn't talking to herself. She was talking to an entity that was able to lure her out of the elevator and ultimately to her death."

That was some heavy stuff.

Kerry looked at the ground, suddenly bashful. I knew this look. She always got it when she wanted to do something that wasn't completely innocent. Kerry was the epitome of a straight-laced goody-goody. But, as is the case with most goody-goodies, when she decided to get up to no good, all hell broke loose. In this case, it would be literal.

"Do you want to try it?" she asked sheepishly, almost whispering, not yet able to bring herself to make eye contact with me. I knew she thought it was a bad idea. But I also knew that her curiosity had gotten the better of her.

The game sounded ridiculous and silly—like something out of a bad comic. But, then again, we were both devout believers in all things paranormal, and I had to admit my curiosity had been piqued. My competitive streak didn't help matters either: if anyone could beat the elevator game and not be lured into another dimension, I was confident that it would be me.

I also had to admit that I was feeling a shameless soft spot for her that would probably be there for the next decade. Almost exactly a year ago, her brother—and my other best friend—had committed suicide. Max. I called him my gay boyfriend, and he was more of a gentleman to me than any of the boys that constituted my lackluster attempts at high school dating had ever been. Many of them called me by the cruel nickname of Olive Oyl since I had her twiggy and less-than-voluptuous physique, her penchant for high collared sack dresses, and her same limp, dark hair pulled into a bun at the nape of the neck. And so, I wasn't particularly popular with the boys. Neither was Kerry. And being the lone out and proud gay student at our tiny Catholic school had made Max somewhat of a pariah. And so, the three of us spent much of our days huddled together in the hallways, seeking shelter from the frostbite of our school's ecosystem, and we spent our weekends doing exactly what Kerry and I found ourselves doing that night: reading magazines, doing crossword puzzles, and surfing the Internet.

Max's death was abrupt and utterly shocking to everyone. I wish I could say that I had seen it coming. But none of us did. Max was almost like a caricature of himself: bouncing around with his exaggerated movements and gravelly, smoke coated voice. Smoking was a habit that he tried to keep hidden by dousing himself in cologne and stuffing his face with mints, but the musky undertones of cigarettes still clung to him.

He was joyful. Or, at least, he did an excellent impression of joyfulness. When he died, phrases like *undiagnosed bipolar disorder* and *untreated mental illness* swarmed around his name like flies when people spoke about him. And those phrases might have been accurate. We would never really know. But I could sense that people hid behind them—cowered, even—as some kind of explanation that would still allow the world to make sense. That would make Max's death more than just an unbearable mystery and a shameful waste. But, for Kerry and me, his absence was like a gushing, irreparable chest wound. It had, of course, given our weekend rituals a deep undercurrent of grief. It penetrated to the molecular level. He was all Kerry and I talked about for the first six months. By the time he had been gone for nine months, we talked about him less and less—a fact which made us almost as sad as losing him in the first place. We commemorated the one-year anniversary of Max's death by watching The Sandlot – his favorite movie—and eating a dozen glazed doughnuts—his favorite guilty pleasure that was always followed by a month of rigorous exercise (we skipped that part). Once a year had come and gone, we seldom spoke about him. It was just too much. The grief seemed to get worse as time went on, and so it was best to just pretend he never existed at all.

In any case, when Kerry made requests of me, I felt compelled to honor them.

I put my hand on Kerry's shoulder and she finally looked at me. I forced a grin, pushing away the thought that Max would have loved to play a game like this.

"Of course I want to try it."

Kerry's father was a contractor who was

working on a massive hotel renovation downtown—
a project about which he had bored her over several
family dinners. He didn't like to talk about Max,
either. Or really anything with emotional substance,
and so he spent meals droning on about work. Kerry
feigned interest about this particular project so that
she could learn about the various intricacies of the
worksite.

The following Friday after deciding we would
play the elevator game, Kerry had managed to
swipe his ID badge from his coat pocket, which
would give us access to the freight elevator in the
half of the building that was closed for construction.
There would be no guests, maids, or managers in
that part of the building, and the construction
workers would have gone home for the day. It
would be just us and whatever creepy spirits might
await.

After telling our parents we were sleeping over
at another friend's house, we hopped into her
crappy brown Honda Civic—nicknamed The Rust
Bucket—and headed downtown. When we arrived
at the hotel, we strolled through the pristine marble
lobby, tapped the ID badge on a door marked
"Employees Only," and walked down a long, dark
hallway illuminated by exit signs. The darkness
combined with the red glow made me wonder if we
weren't already in a different dimension.

We reached a wide-open area that was still
unfinished. Buckets and tools were scattered
haphazardly as if the workers chose to drop
everything right at quitting time. The lights were on
but not yet working at their full capacity and they

flickered erratically. We walked past a bank of passenger elevators to the freight elevator, and Kerry tapped the ID badge to another pad before pressing the call button. The elevator clanked and whirred, emitting creaking sounds indicative of neglect. When it reached the bottom, the door strained open with a growl. It was as if we were at the maw of a broken, elderly beast. The adrenaline was starting to build. There were few things in life that I liked more than a hit of adrenaline. It was an addiction, and I had a feeling that whether the elevator game was real or not, I was about to go on a bender. I took a step forward and felt Kerry pull on my arm.

"Wait. What if all of this is, like, for real?" She looked down at her feet. I could tell her fear was embarrassing to her in that moment, as, like me, fear usually tended to excite and motivate her. After all, we were the girls at the slumber party who insisted on a horror movie marathon, who played Bloody Mary in dark bathrooms, and who whipped out the Ouija Board whenever we had the opportunity (including one time in a cemetery at midnight). In fact, just like the cemetery Ouija Board session, this whole thing had been Kerry's idea, but I knew she was getting cold feet.

"Isn't that why we are here?" I coaxed. "To see if it's for real?" I could feel my adrenaline starting to fade, and I didn't like it. We had come this far. I was going to play this game.

"Yes, but..." she twirled a piece of hair around her finger and wouldn't look at me. "What if there *really is* another dimension and we get stuck in it?

Is it smart for both of us to be in there together?"

I looked at her and sighed. I had been equally terrified when we did the Ouija Board on top of a tombstone, but I had enjoyed every minute of it. I was getting the sense that Kerry's relationship to fear might be slightly different, and perhaps more reasonable, than mine. Kerry was the kind of person who could be, as I called her, "consistently inconsistent." One minute, she was enthusiastic about something, and the next, it was like she wanted to lie down and take a nap. Her energy levels and overall demeanor were not unlike my elderly basset hound. I gave her the same sympathetic look that I often gave my dog and decided to let her off the hook.

"You're right. Maybe one of us should keep watch. Maybe you should stay. If someone asks why you're here, you can always show your dad's ID and make up a cover story. Tell him he sent you to find his lost car keys or something." I smiled at my ingenuity and checked in with myself to see if I still wanted to proceed. I certainly did. I was more like my Russian Blue cat, who could seldom be swayed once she locked onto a target.

I could see the relief on Kerry's face. "Besides," I said, giving her a nudge, "I'm pretty sure this whole thing is a bunch of BS anyway."

I stepped into the elevator and looked at my forearm. I had scrawled the floor sequence on it in Sharpie: 1, 4, 2, 6, 2, 10, 5, 1.

"Let's see. First stop, fourth floor! Women's lingerie!"

Kerry ignored my joke and pointed her index

finger at me.

"Remember," she said, "do not talk to or look at the woman who enters the elevator. Do not get off the elevator if anything seems strange. I mean, *anything*—even if it's something small like a weird smell, stay in the elevator. You will know that you are in the other dimension when everything is dark and you see the red cross. Do not interact with anyone you see. And, no matter what, you have to finish the game and get back to the ground floor."

As the doors closed, I gave her a salute to let her know her message had been received. We had agreed that if anything went wrong, I would hit the emergency bell. Hopefully, she would be able to hear it in her dimension. The elevator began moving, and I felt the adrenaline that had gone stagnant during our conversation begin to rise again. There was a part of me that had a feeling that the game wouldn't work. A bigger part of me, however, hoped that it would.

Just as long as you're careful, everything will be fine, I told myself. I knew the rules and planned on following them. I was ready to enjoy whatever good scares might be in store for me.

The elevator announced its arrival at the fourth floor with a *thunk* and an off-key *ping.* I patted its wall to encourage it.

The doors opened. Just like the lobby below, a half-lit, half-finished hallway stretched before me. Buckets, tools, and drop cloths covered the floor. There was nothing to see here. I looked at my arm.

"Next stop, second floor! Men's department!"

I laughed at my own joke. Once again, the

freight elevator groaned and shuddered on its way to the second floor. When the doors opened, I saw that the hallway was fully finished. Only one light was on, but the slick new floor reflected it brightly. Brass fixtures and cherry wood covered every surface. I pressed the button again, this time for the sixth floor. When the doors opened, I gasped.

A woman was standing there.

"Oh, thank goodness," she said as she entered the elevator. "I got lost in this maze of a hotel and wound up in a construction zone where none of the other elevators were working! Can you tell me how to get to the fitness center?"

I remembered Kerry's stern warning and did not look at or speak to the woman. I could tell in my peripheral vision that she was wearing workout clothes and carrying a yoga mat. I said nothing and pressed the button for the second floor.

"Excuse me? Did you hear me?"

I said nothing and stared at the floor.

"Are you deaf or something?"

She moved to stand in front of me. I turned away.

"What is your problem?"

I said nothing. When the elevator reached the second floor, I closed my eyes and gestured to the hallway, hoping she would think I was directing her to the fitness center and leave the elevator. She disembarked, muttering curse words under her breath. I kept my eyes closed until the doors closed again so that I did not risk catching a glimpse.

I felt a little silly. The rational part of my brain told me that this woman was just lost and searching for her yoga class, not trying to lure me into another dimension. However, the part of my brain that believed in the supernatural—and, I'll admit, that part constituted the majority—thought it was always better to be safe than sorry. I shook off my uncomfortable feelings and pressed the button for the tenth floor. The elevator whirred and clunked, but when it reached its destination the doors stayed closed. Great. The big metal dinosaur had chosen *that moment* to go extinct. I pressed the button for the doors to open. Nothing happened. Not good.

"Look, I know this game is stupid, but I have to finish it. Please help me and I promise to make sure to put in a good word for you to Kerry's dad." I patted the wall. "You know, so they don't send you to the scrap heap, or Elevator Heaven, or whatever it is that they do with old guys like you."

My pleading seemed to work because a moment later the doors heaved open. Like the others, the hallway was only half-lit and littered with construction debris. A sheet of plastic hung over the window at— the end, and in front of it, I saw the silhouette of a figure. It was petite and almost frail-looking, and it began walking toward me. It stepped into a pool of overhead light partway down the hallway and I could make out a familiar floral pattern on her blouse, like something a substitute teacher would wear. It was Kerry! She must have come looking for me and taken the stairs.

I left the elevator and ran into the hallway.

"Kerry! I'm so happy to see you! The elevator is stuck. Do you have your dad's—"

Kerry was reaching out to me, beckoning me

21

with her fingers. She began making strange squeaking sounds, and I ran to be closer to her.

Her eyes and lips were sewn shut with a thick, ropy thread. I stood there, staring in disbelief as she—this *thing*—inched closer to me. It had Kerry's face and body, but it was not Kerry.

"Oh my God...."

Heat shot up my spine and into my scalp, and my skin started to prickle. I turned and ran back to the elevator. Before I reached it, something grabbed my arm, digging into it with sharp nails. I didn't dare look back. I wriggled my way out of my cardigan to escape whatever was gripping me and ducked inside the elevator, hiding by the control panel and pressing the door close button.

"Come on, come on..." I pleaded, panting. I was scared, and not the fun kind of scared. A pale hand reached into the elevator a second before the doors closed and then retracted. A solitary bang against the door from the outside reverberated through the elevator and then everything was silent.

What the hell was that? I had clearly seen a bizarro Kerry from another dimension. But it was nothing like accounts of playing the elevator game that I had read on the Internet. There were no mentions of doppelgangers. There had been light in the hallway and no red cross. I was thoroughly shaken. This no longer felt like just a fun game, and I was beginning to suspect that it wasn't just a silly Internet legend. I needed to finish the sequence and get out of wherever I was.

I looked down at my arm again and pressed the fifth floor. The elevator complied, albeit not without some graceless jolting. It took a few moments for me to realize I had been holding my breath. I had no idea what to expect next.

The elevator stopped at the fifth floor. I hid by the control panel—it wasn't lost on me that the woman in the red raincoat from the elevator video had hidden in just the same way—as the doors opened. I was expecting blackness when I finally peeked around the corner. Instead, the hallway had the same layout as all the others, but it was drenched in a cloying shade of pink. It reminded me of the time I splattered my white bedroom walls with recently swallowed Pepto Bismol during a bout of the stomach flu. There were frilly curtains over the window at the end of the hallway and paintings of carousel horses. It was like a Victorian nursery. It didn't belong here.

The noise was faint at first—barely perceptible. A giggle. And then the echoing of footsteps. They were small and quick as if they belonged to a child. And then louder giggling and more footsteps. I stepped one foot out of the elevator and was almost bowled over by a child running past me and down another section of the hallway. Then, silence. I pulled my foot back into the elevator. All I could hear was my own breath.

One of the doors lining the hallway opened, and a little girl stepped out of it. Her face was hidden by her hands, but I could hear sobs. She was crying. She wore a lacy pinafore, patent leather Mary Janes, and had blond ringlets like an antique doll.

"She's looking for you!" Her words were muffled by her hands. She let them fall to her sides, and I could see that her face was wet. Pouring from her eyes were not tears, but blood.

The rest of the doors opened all at once. In an instant, the hallway was filled with children. They were running erratically, bumping into each other and the wall as if they were blind. The little girls looked just like the one who had spoken to me. She was standing in the middle of it all, staring at me with her ghastly, blood-covered face. The boys were wearing knickers and white collared shirts as if they were about to head to an old-fashioned church. Their charming appearances made the whole scene even more confusing. I felt a whimper build in my throat, and all I could do was watch as these children ran around the hallway. I couldn't get my arm to do what I was commanding it to do: push the "door close" button. After a few minutes, when my arm finally decided to comply, I pounded the button frantically.

Please, please, please. C'mon….

Suddenly, the footsteps in the hallway stopped. I lifted my eyes from the control panel. The children had their backs to me. There was a buzzing sound, like a broken fluorescent bulb. A loud squealing note exploded in my ear, and I put a hand over it in an attempt to stifle it.

Ever so slowly, the children turned around in unison, as if they were on rotating bases. Now I understood why they had bumped into each other. Their eyes were empty sockets, and from them, black blood poured down their faces. They stood still, like dolls on a shelf, waiting to be played with. Terrible, horrifying dolls. The air became shrill with laughter and all at once, their little feet began running toward me. Of their own accord, the elevator doors slammed with more speed than I thought possible, just before the children could reach me. It was as if the elevator was protecting me. The children's tiny fists banged on the door, and the sound echoed like demonic raindrops.

I pressed the button for the first floor, moved to the back corner, and huddled into a ball. The fear had rooted into every part of my body and I began to sweat and shake. My heart and breath were too fast and I couldn't slow them down.

"It's ok, it's ok. You just need to get back to the first floor and the game will be over. Just one more floor." I rested my face on my knees and covered my ears with my hands. The elevator lurched and jolted, making its troublesome noises one last time. I felt it come to a stop and heard the doors open. I was expecting to see Kerry, waiting for me. She wasn't. I burst into tears.

Standing outside the elevator doors was Max. He wasn't supposed to be here. But I didn't care. The one thing I had wished for in the past year was to throw my arms around him one more time. To smell him and look at him and share all of the times I had said to myself, "Max would love this." But most of all, I wanted a break from the constant and relentless grief that had flowed like hot magma through my life since his death.

"Oh my God, oh my God..." I ran into his arms, sobbing. "I miss you and love you so much...."

"Shhhh..." he whispered into my hair. His

25

breath was warm and he smelled like cigarettes masked with cologne. Just like he always had. We stood there, clutching each other.

I extracted my face from the puddle I had created on his shirt and looked at him. He always smiled so widely that it made his eyes squint and the skin around them crinkle. I had missed those eyes. His auburn hair was still a mop of curls on his head.

"You shouldn't be here...". I touched his face, slurring my words through the tears.

"No, sweetie. *You* shouldn't be here. This place isn't safe for you. Why are you here?"

"Kerry and I wanted to see what would happen...". I suddenly felt silly and hugged him again. "If you had been here, you would have wanted to play the game too. Knowing this made me miss you even more."

"Oh, Alice. This isn't a Ouija Board. This game is dangerous." He chuckled sweetly. "And yes, I would have wanted to play, but *you* should know better. And I miss you, too. But listen carefully: we need to get you out of here."

He pulled back from our embrace and looked at me, smiling, with his eyes squinting.

I smiled back, my eyes filling with tears.

And then the smile left. In a quick motion, his arm moved and I felt a searing pain across my throat. My hand instinctively covered it and became hot with liquid. It pulsated and spilled down the front of my shirt, and I slid down the back wall of the elevator as the blood darkened my clothing and began to spread to the floor around me. I closed my eyes so that I couldn't see Max. I knew it wasn't him. Just like it hadn't been Kerry.

I was choking and gasping. Air became elusive, and a gargling sound grew in the back of my throat. It wouldn't be long now.

"See ya, Spook," he said.

Spook had been Max's nickname for me. That one hurt.

The ground spun for a moment, and then it was as if the elevator bottom had dropped out and I was falling quickly into nothingness. My breath jolted and rattled one last time. And then, silence.

Someone was shaking me.

"Alice! Alice! Can you hear me?" I opened my eyes and saw Kerry—whose mouth and eyes were *not* stitched shut—sitting next to me. I touched my throat. It was fully intact.

"What happened?" I croaked out. Even though my throat was whole, my voice seemed damaged. That didn't make sense.

Kerry helped me to my feet. "I don't know. You were gone for a really long time, and when the doors opened you were on the ground, unconscious."

I felt a flutter of panic where the wound on my throat had been. I brought my hand to it. "Kerry, we have to get out of here. Now."

"Just tell me you're ok."

"I don't know. Let's just go." My knees were weak, and it was hard for me to walk. Kerry put my arm over her shoulder.

It wasn't until we stepped from the elevator that

I saw that the lights were off and the hallway was pitch black. I stopped.

Kerry felt me tense up and rubbed my back. "I know what you're thinking, but it's ok. All of the lights are out on this side of the building. I think they turn them off around 2 a.m. There's no point in keeping them on all night, I guess. I was so worried that the elevator wouldn't work. Thank goodness you made it back safely."

My legs felt detached from my body and I had to look down at my feet to make sure they were moving. I just wanted to get as far away from that elevator as I could. I wanted to get to a place where there was light, and people, and maybe some strong coffee. I needed to tell Kerry everything that had happened in the game. And that it wasn't just a game at all. I kept my eyes on the exit. Nothing else mattered.

Sometimes in our haste to move forward, we miss things. Fine details, nuances, slippery twists of fate. Often we ignore these things at our peril. I was moving with a singular focus along a straight line toward the door. Safety was just a few steps away.

What I didn't see, there in the darkness just outside my field of vision, was a glowing red cross.

The Three Kings Game

Do not play this game.

This is the disclaimer at the top of every Internet article written about the Three Kings Game. Just before they list step-by-step instructions and rules, they make sure to tell the reader to NEVER, EVER, EVER play this game. It's too dangerous.

Unfortunately, the money was too good.

It was a gloomy day, which, in retrospect, was kind of perfect, when my phone rang. "Hey, Beth, are you ready to work?" That's what my editor at *The Muse Magazine*—the voice on the other end of the phone—always said when he had an article for me to write. Since becoming a freelance writer three years ago, I had been published in dozens of places. Of all of them, *The Muse* was my favorite. It explored the quirkier side of pop culture, often capitalizing on humanity's sense of morbid curiosity. We can't seem to help ourselves. The last article I wrote for them was about cremation jewelry: Turn your loved ones into diamonds and wear them forever! It went viral and briefly kicked off a trend. The idea made me sick to my stomach, but I loved the brief moment of Internet fame (and the paycheck) that had accompanied it.

"At your service, Joe. What do you have for me?"

"Someone sent in a YouTube video of a girl playing what is known as the Three Kings Game. Ever heard of it?"

"Can't say I have."

"Ok. Well, the basic premise is that, by following the steps of a ritual involving two chairs and a mirror at 3:33 a.m., you can summon evil spirits. I guess they come from a place called The Shadowside, or something like that."

"Ok…is that it?"

"Yeah."

"So, that begs the question: Why would anyone want to do something like that?"

Joe chuckled. He was used to my questions. "Why does anyone do any of this stuff? Because they're curious. Because they want inarguable proof that the spirit realm exists. Because they haven't gotten laid in a while."

"Real nice, Joe."

"Anyway, a girl made a YouTube video of herself playing the game. In the mirrors that she has set up, you can see some dark figures, and you hear her scream before falling to the floor. And then you see a dark figure pass in front of the camera as if it has come out of the mirror. If you listen carefully, you can hear…a strange noise."

"A strange noise?"

"Yeah…it can best be described as, uh, a giggle. Honestly, it's pretty freaky sounding. Then you hear her friend call her name, run into the room, and throw a bucket of water on her. The girl on the floor doesn't move, and the friend is looking around frantically. Then she looks into the camera and says, 'she's here, she's here. If you're watching this, it's too late for us.' And then the video goes dark."

"So, what happened to them?"

"Well, that's the thing. Everyone thinks it's just a run-of-the-mill, staged video designed for social media attention, but I happen to know that both of those girls are in the hospital. They're completely catatonic. Neither one has spoken since that night."

"How did they post the video?"

"Good question. No one knows. But one of their friends found them right after she watched the video. Luckily they had left the door unlocked. They were both unconscious, and the friend called 911."

"Can you verify that this report of their condition is accurate?" I couldn't help but proudly flip my hair over my shoulder. I loved acting like a hard-nosed journalist, even if it was for a puff piece.

"Yes, actually."

"By whom?"

Joe exhaled audibly. I knew it wasn't going to be the head of neurology.

"I spoke to an orderly who works at the hospital. He was able to confirm that the story was true."

"Was he cleaning their bedpans?" I chuckled. Joe ignored me. "Alright, so would you like me to investigate this story? Do a little digging and find out more about the girls and what really happened that night?"

"No." Once again, he exhaled audibly. I knew a big ask was coming. "I want you to play The Three Kings Game."

When we hung up twenty minutes later, he had convinced me to write the story, and I had

31

convinced him to pay me an extra fifty cents per word. If I played my cards right and added the occasional unnecessary adjective, I would be able to make a big dent in this month's rent. I threw my comforter off, sending my phone and laptop sailing. I had taken this call in bed, just like I had taken all of my calls for the past few weeks. And meals. I would have taken my showers there too if I could. But then again, I couldn't remember the last time I had taken a shower. The nice thing about being a freelance writer is that showering and wearing pants are optional. I opened the door from my bedroom—which only fit a bed and a side table—to the rest of the apartment and noticed the difference in temperature and smell. I hadn't left my bedroom all morning, and the rest of my Manhattan shoebox suddenly seemed enormous. I was also acutely aware that my bedroom smelled like body odor.

The bedroom door opened into a short, narrow hallway just across from my apartment door. The hallway led to my living room, a corner of which was taken up with what could technically be called a kitchen. It was what was known in New York City real estate as an "efficiency kitchen," which meant that the refrigerator was dorm-room sized, and the stove was essentially a glorified hot plate.

I grabbed a bottle of water from the fridge and saw the half-drunk bottle of chardonnay that had been last night's companion.

"Well, it's after 12…" I uncorked it and took several hearty swallows, which I chased with a handful of popcorn. *There,* I thought. *That should tide me over long enough to do some preliminary research.* I changed into a fresh set of sweats—cringing a little as I pulled on my Yale sweatshirt, as I didn't feel worthy of it at that moment—and crawled back into bed. I pulled my laptop over the comforter and propped myself up on pillows.

I Googled The Three Kings Game, chose one of the many posts about it, and after scrolling past multiple warnings about the game's dangers, I found the instructions:

1. Place a chair in the middle of a quiet, empty room, facing north. Place two more chairs opposite that chair, facing it. The first chair is the throne. The other two are the Queen and Fool chairs.

2. Place two large mirrors on the Queen and Fool chairs, and angle them so that they are both facing the throne and each other. The throne should be reflected in both mirrors.

3. Place a bucket of water and a mug in front of the throne. This is one fail-safe.

4. Place a fan behind the throne and turn it on. This is another fail-safe.

5. Go to your bedroom, put an unlit candle by the bed, set your alarm for 3:30 a.m., and hold a power object—something from your childhood, such as a stuffed animal. This is a third fail-safe, and it will guide you back to your true self if something goes wrong.

6. When the alarm goes off at 3:30 a.m., you have three minutes exactly to grab the candle and be seated, with the power object, in the throne. You must be seated by 3:33 a.m., or else you cannot proceed with the game. You also must make sure that the fan is still on. If everything is in order, light the candle. Look straight ahead into the darkness—no matter what, do not look at the mirrors. You are the King. You will not know which chair is for the Queen and which is for the Fool. You will be summoning entities from what is called The Shadowside. And, from their perspective, you will either be their Queen or their Fool—hence the name Three Kings. They will make their presence known to you by manifesting in the mirrors or speaking. At 4:34 a.m.—not a minute sooner—you can blow out the candle and the game will end.

Well. This all seemed simple enough. There was, however, a list of disclaimers longer than the one I read when Joe sent me on an extreme spelunking expedition:

If your alarm doesn't go off at 3:30, if you are not seated by 3:33, or the fan is turned off, abort the mission. Leave your apartment and do not return until after 6:00 a.m.

If anything should happen to your body during the ritual, the fan will blow out the candle and the ritual will end, bringing you back to safety.

You should have a loved one on standby in another room who can call your phone at 4:34 a.m. If you do not answer, she should call your name. If you still do not answer, she should enter the room and, without touching you, throw the bucket of water on you.

The post didn't say what would happen if all of those safety measures were to fail.

I did a quick mental scan: I had an alarm, a power object, chairs, candle, and a fan. What I didn't have were mirrors or someone who would be willing to come over at 4:34 a.m. Since separating from my husband and moving to my divorcée palace uptown, I had been avoiding both mirrors and human contact beyond what was required for basic survival or paying my bills. I didn't want to see my failures—and dramatic weight gain— reflected back at me. And I couldn't bear to hear the twinge of pity in everyone's voice over the phone.

It was all so terribly cliché. He had run off with his secretary (or, well, she preferred the term "executive assistant"). I couldn't decide what was more unbearable: my heartbreak or how utterly unoriginal the cause of it was. If I was going to be dumped and shattered, the least he could have done was run off to Africa to save babies or decide to take a vow of silence and become a monk. Anything but his *secretary.* I seem to have responded by becoming a cliché myself: the depressed, divorced journalist, living in a small-yet-expensive apartment, subsisting on a diet of popcorn and chardonnay. I had been a student leader in college, a trailblazing writer in my 20s, and a thriving socialite until just a few months ago. If the younger versions of myself could see the pitiful sad sack I had become, they would hang their heads in shame. Or kick my ass. Or both. I had at least managed to escape with some valuable first edition books, several Burmese rubies we acquired on a trip to Asia, and a rare violin – worth a lot of money – that was collecting dust under my bed until I could find the will to part with it. And when the lawyers were finished with him, there would be a hefty financial settlement that would be sufficient enough for me to move into a much nicer place. So I guess my pain was worth something. I did, however, leave my dignity with the doorman on the way out.

I ordered mirrors from Amazon and sent the invoice to Joe. One problem was solved. However, I still didn't know who would rescue me at 4:34 a.m., and the sad reality of my loneliness could only be assuaged by taking a half-hour nap. When I awoke, I had a flash of inspiration. I picked up my phone and called Rosie.

Rosie and I had worked together in the New York offices of a shamelessly trashy British tabloid before she decided she was above this line of work and moved back to her native London. She would be the perfect person to call because she was nothing if not punctual and reliable. And, at 4:34 a.m. New York time, it would be 9:34 a.m. London time. She would just be settling into her workday.

The phone did that weird double ring thing that it does whenever you call another country.

"Hello?"

"Hey, Rosie. It's Beth Carpenter."

"Oh, Beth. You've been on my mind. I'm so sorry about Andy. How are you getting on?"

I cringed. Her voice was practically oozing with pity. "I'm taking him to the cleaners—don't you worry." She laughed the way you do when you're both affectionately amused but also slightly embarrassed for someone. "Listen, I need a favor. I'm working on a story, and I know this may sound weird, but can you call my cell phone on Wednesday morning at exactly 9:34 your time?"

"Ok...do I need to tell you anything in particular when I call? I know that you get up to some strange things over there at *The Muse*. They're not trying to test your fear of small spaces again, are they?"

"No. Ha. Nothing like that. Just make sure I answer. And if I don't, can you call my boss? Just ask him to come over and check on me."

"Um...are you sure you're all right, Beth?"

"Yes, of course."

"Are you...thinking of harming yourself? That balding prick isn't worth it!"

"Come on, Rosie. No. My boss asked me to do an assignment, and it needs to be submitted by exactly 4:34 a.m. on Wednesday morning. That's all. You're just holding me accountable."

"Alright then. If you're sure..."

It took another ten minutes to convince Rosie that I didn't need to be placed on suicide watch. She finally agreed to call me, which meant that I had my safety net in place. She wouldn't be able to throw a bucket of water on me, but I was fairly confident that it wouldn't be necessary.

I hadn't told Joe this, but the few times I had attempted games like this, I had failed pretty spectacularly. I had tried the Ouija Board at countless sleepovers, only to have the planchette stay stock still. I had always been the one person no one could lift during Light as a Feather, Stiff as a Board, and even my best friend who claimed to have conjured Bloody Mary numerous times was unsuccessful when I was in the room. It wasn't that I was a non-believer—I was open to the possibility that ghosts were real. It's just that something about me seemed to repel the spirit world.

On Tuesday the mirrors arrived, and I got to work shoving my cheap Ikea furniture against the wall. He had kept all the good stuff, plus I had no interest in the couch where he and the secretary had consummated their relationship. I also re-read the game instructions several times so that I wouldn't miss a step. The actual setup for the ritual—I had decided to refer to it as a ritual as opposed to a game since it seemed to be a bit more serious than Uno on a Friday night—should, according to the directions, happen no sooner than 11 p.m., which meant that I had four hours to binge-watch *The Great British Baking Show*. I was still a sucker for all things British. At 11 p.m. sharp, I set up the chairs, mirror, and fan. I decided to skip the bucket of water since there was no one to throw it on me. When I stepped back to examine the scene, I saw something that terrified me to my core: my own reflection. My sweats were tight on me, giving the weight I had gained nowhere to hide. My waist-length blond hair—always my best feature—was riddled with split ends and my roots were damp with grease. I had somehow managed to maintain porcelain skin throughout my life – my face had remained pimple-free in my teen years, and was wrinkle-free now – but the face looking back at me was puffy and pale. My blue eyes seemed dull. Ugh. I couldn't believe I let my heartbreak have this much power over me.

After turning on the fan and turning off the lights in the living room, I crawled back into bed, set the alarm for 3:30 a.m., and grabbed my power object—the teddy bear named Fritz that I got for my seventh birthday. I chuckled at the fact that he was supposed to bring me back to myself in the midst of darkness and evil. Hopefully, it would prove to be that simple.

3:30 a.m. I tucked Fritz under my arm, gathered the lighter and candle I had left on the nightstand, and used the glow of my phone to light my way to the living room. I managed to shut my bedroom door, light the candle, and be seated by 3:32 a.m. The fan had stayed on. Perfect. I could proceed.

On the wall across from me was a vintage poster I had gotten from a big box store in an effort to make my place homier. It was a harlequin drinking some kind of Italian spirit. I stared at it, not allowing my eyes to drift to either mirror (as instructed by the rules), though they wanted to. The harlequin seemed to move and shift the longer I stared as my eyes played tricks in the candlelight.

Hisssss. Clank. The steam in the radiator grew restless, causing me to jump. My hearing seemed to take on an almost animal-like keenness—I could hear all of the tiny sounds around me, even the ones that were usually drowned out by the sounds of traffic ten stories below. A scrape here, a scurry there. I made a mental note to call my super about mice.

I was trying to focus on the noises not because I was waiting for something to appear from The Shadowside, but because I found silence unbearable. Silence is absence. It is my dad's empty closet after he left. I sat inside of it for an entire day, my six-year-old-self trying to summon him back. It is the moment at my mother's funeral after the last note of her favorite hymn ended. It is the sound of an Upper East Side apartment that I wished hadn't been so big once my marriage was no longer taking up space inside of it. It is the phone that rang for weeks with sympathetic calls after my separation, and then, when the rings went unanswered, became mute.

My apartment seemed alive with sounds, and I could hear the ceaseless motion of the city outside. But there were no strange voices, and nothing was flashing in my peripheral vision. No one was appearing in the mirrors.

I was completely alone.

The phone rang at 4:34 a.m., right on the dot.

"Hi, Rosie."

"Not swinging from the rafters, are you?"

"No. Ha. I promise you, I'm fine."

"Ok. Ring me when it's a more reasonable hour where you are. And get some sleep."

"I will. Thanks."

I blew out the candle, shut off the fan, and turned on the lights. Nothing had happened, which was exactly what I had anticipated.

"Well, Fritz, let's go to bed. I'll figure out what to tell Joe later today." I tucked him under my arm and walked to my bedroom door.

It was open. That was strange. I was certain I had closed it.

My ringtone woke me up. I picked up my phone. It was 1 p.m. No doubt it was Joe checking in about the story and making sure I hadn't been dragged to another dimension by a malevolent spirit. I cleared my throat and did my best impression of someone who hadn't just woken up.

"Hello?!"

Static.

"Hello? Joe?"

More static. And then a giggle. A voice hissed in my ear:

Chess piece, card deck, stolen tart
Shards of glass will fall apart.
Mirror, mirror
Thrones of three,
Look behind you,
Who is she?

More giggling. More static. And then nothing. Joe was quite the practical joker, but this little prank call was not his finest work. I clicked on recent calls, but the only information it provided was *No Caller ID.* Great. I clicked on Joe's number.

"Hello?"

"The answer is the Queen of Hearts. That one was pretty obvious."

"Beth? Is that you? What are you talking about?"

"Nice try. The riddle that you or someone you put up to asked me to answer."

"Uh…." He was silent, which was unusual for him. "Honestly, I have no idea what you are talking about. Listen, are you ok?"

I rolled my eyes. He wasn't going to let me have this one.

"Yes. I'm fine."

"Good. I'm glad you called. I've been dying to hear how the game went. Did you summon any spirits?"

"It was uneventful. Unfortunately, The Shadowside didn't take much of an interest in me."

Again, that audible exhale. It was quite the trademark. "That's disappointing. Ok, plan b: why don't you see if you can contact someone who *did* have a strange experience. People chat about these things in forums all the time. Get a few quotes and then write it up."

"No problem, boss."

"Great."

"And that riddle was way too easy."

Brief pause. Again, Joe rarely paused.

"I still have no idea what you are talking about. Are you sure you're ok?"

I knew he didn't really want the true answer to that question. I was starting to think that he hadn't been the one calling me. If it had been him, he wouldn't be able to resist taking credit.

"I'm fine."

"Ok," he said, uncertainly. "Get to work, and we will touch base later."

I clicked my phone off. If that call didn't come

from Joe, who had called me? No one other than him knew I was playing the Three Kings Game, or would have any idea about the mirrors or thrones of three. *What was happening?* Maybe I had been half asleep when I answered the phone and had dreamt the whole thing. I decided not to check my call log in the event that it would refute that theory. I pulled the covers over my head and felt a panicked tightening in my chest. It was two feelings together: fight-or-flight meets dread. It was unfamiliar and physically uncomfortable, and I vowed to stay under the covers until the feelings passed.

But then I heard the sound of glass breaking in the next room. I flung the covers off and quickly scanned the bedroom for something I could use as a weapon. My hardcover copy of *Infinite Jest* was the closest thing I could reach. Getting hit on the head with that tome could surely do some damage.

I opened the bedroom door slowly, expecting to see a masked intruder looking around disappointedly at the meager offerings of my apartment. Instead, the room was empty. The air felt too still. Something wasn't right.

One of the mirrors had toppled off of its chair and was lying face down on the floor. I righted it again but cracks crisscrossed it like lines on a subway map, leaving my reflection distorted. I couldn't help but reach out and touch it, tracing my finger along the veins of breakage. It's strange that mirrors have complete control over how we see ourselves. Sometimes my reflection feels more real than I do.

"Ouch!"

I cut my finger on an errant splinter of glass, and a small drop of blood trickled down the mirror. I watched it for a moment before something else caught my attention. Another reflection.

I whirled around, but no one was there. When I turned back to the mirror, the reflection was gone. It happened too quickly for me to be sure what exactly I had seen, and the image of the woman had been refracted by the shattered mirror. But I was sure of two things: she was wearing red, and her face had been a shock of white.

I decided to throw out both mirrors, put away the fan, and move the chairs back where they belonged. I figured that this would be enough to get rid of the woman in red. But just in case, I retreated to my bedroom and locked the door.

"Stay calm," I told myself. "You followed the rules and nothing appeared during the game. All of this is in your imagination."

The glow of my laptop was strangely comforting as if I had a friend in the room. I began my fishing expedition for *The Muse* story by visiting forums. Many people shared that they had gone into trances during the game and had to utilize the back-up person and bucket of water. Others had seen shadows and heard noises, like growling, singing, and an unsettling giggle. Reading about the giggle put an acidic ball into my stomach. I had also heard a giggle, and it had been menacing. But why hadn't I heard it during the game? And, more importantly, how could I make sure I never heard it again?

I opened up a Google Doc and began typing.

After an hour, the clacking of the keyboard was joined by another, quieter sound. It was barely perceptible, but I stopped typing and listened. It was a faint scratching sound, and at first, I thought it was the mice. But then I realized that the scratches weren't random. They seemed to have shape and substance. It took a few moments for my brain to place the sound.

It was writing. Someone was writing on my bedroom door. It sounded like something was being scrawled with a quill, moving with an effort not required by a ballpoint pen. With one final pronounced scratch, the writing stopped. I pulled Fritz—my power object—to my chest.

The fear was like a hand on the back of my head, and it stroked its fingers down to my lower back, spreading goosebumps along the way. I knew I needed to go and see what was on the other side of that door, but I really didn't want to. I thought about calling my super and asking him to enter the apartment and check for me, but I would feel silly if it turned out to be nothing. I didn't need yet another person looking at me with pitying eyes.

I slid my laptop off of me, tucked Fritz under one arm and *Infinite Jest* under the other, and clambered over my bed to the door. I held my breath and put my hand on the knob for just a moment, gathering my courage, before turning it.

The opposite side of the door was covered in erratic, manic script. The ink dripped down it the way my blood had dripped down the mirror.

She shows your true face

And tells no lie
On the Ides
The King must die

A wave of dizziness hit me. I ran out of my apartment and into the hallway. I started to run toward the elevator when I realized I had nowhere to go. I couldn't run to a friend's apartment looking like this. What would I tell them? That I was being terrorized by spirits? I couldn't go to a coffee shop either; I didn't even have shoes on nor had I grabbed my purse. I couldn't knock on a neighbor's door, as I was friendly with none of them, not being the kind that was prone to small talk in the elevator—none of them even knew my name. I sat on the ground. I was alone. And there was something terrible in my apartment.

Fritz and the book were still under my arms, and I moved Fritz to face me and looked into his button eyes. He had been the most consistent male presence in my life, and that thought turned my stomach. I thought briefly about my ex and his secretary lounging around on our expensive furniture in my former (expensive) apartment. My current apartment wasn't much to look at (or smell), but it was mine. It was something in the world that I had sought out and earned. It belonged to me.

"No." I said to Fritz. "This is our apartment. I was already chased out of the last one. I'm not getting chased out of this one, too." I grabbed the spare key from the top of the doorframe and let myself back in. I dropped Fritz and my book by the door and raised my fists into a fighting stance. I waited.

The giggling came from everywhere at once. I peed my sweats a little before pulling myself together.

"Giggles and riddles," I yelled at the air. "You must be the Fool." The giggling stopped. I thought about what I had seen in the mirror. Dressed in red. That was the Queen. Which meant I was the King.

I looked at the riddle on the door again. "On the Ides, the King must die," I read to myself. I remembered from my tenth grade Shakespeare class that the Ides refers to either the 13th or 15th, depending upon how many days were in a particular month. It was November, which has 30 days, which meant that the Ides would be on the 13th. I took a breath. Today was the 11th. I had time to figure all this out.

The sun was beginning to think about setting, and usually, I loved how the light looked in my apartment at that time of day. This time, however, it carried with it a sense of foreboding, that just behind it, something was waiting. It would be dark soon.

I flipped on all of the lights and lit every single candle I could find, hoping to flood my apartment with brightness. But the mingling aromas—for most of the candles were scented—made the air an unpleasant potpourri, and the amassed candlelight seemed almost fragile as if it was not strong enough to absorb the encroaching darkness. I picked up Fritz from where I had left him on the floor, and sat in a chair, holding him on my lap. I waited. For what, I wasn't sure. When it was finally night, the sky outside my window was viscous and thick, like molasses had been poured over my apartment building. The familiar traffic sounds were muffled, and even the searing electricity of the city's lights couldn't seem to make its way into the room. Everything was eerily dark and still. I felt the small hairs on my body perk up like someone had held a staticky balloon just above them.

When glass breaks, it makes a sharp crystalline sound that is almost musical. It was not a sound I was expecting to hear. One by one, the windows began to shatter into small spiderwebs as if they had been punched. First, the window over the kitchen sink, followed by one window in the living room, and then the other. From where I sat, I could also hear the windows in the bedroom breaking. With each punch, my body spasmed, like my own bones were taking the blows.

"Shards of glass will fall apart...holy shit." I found myself whispering. And then—all at once—darkness. The lights and candles had been suddenly extinguished, and the air seemed thin and scarce. It was like a coffin. My nerves were sizzling in panic and my heart lurched in my chest, propelling me into action. I still clutched Fritz as I ran to my apartment door, as all of my earlier arguments for holding my ground had evaporated. Somehow, I knew I wouldn't be able to open the door, even before trying the knob. I dropped Fritz and pulled with both hands, but it still wouldn't open.

I turned around and ran into my bedroom, where I wrestled with the unwashed tangle of sheets until they finally regurgitated my phone and laptop.

The phone, in spite of having been fully charged, was dead. Upon opening the laptop, its faithful glow greeted me. I clicked on my e-mail, and my hands were shaking so uncontrollably I could barely type my message to Joe: *The game is real. There's something in my apartment. It won't let me out. I'm scared. I need you to come over.* And then, because I knew he wouldn't believe me: *I swear on my dead mother's grave that I am telling the truth.* I hit send and my eyes darted to the top of the screen.

No. It couldn't be.

The date read November 13th. How was that possible?

I felt dizzy. I pulled up Google and then one website after another. November 13th, over and over again.

"No, no, no, no….." *On the Ides, the King must die.*

I pulled up my e-mail again. This time I e-mailed my entire contact list with a single word: HELP.

I turned my laptop around so that the screen was facing away from me in an attempt to light the room. My breath was coming so hard and fast that I had to open my mouth and fill the room with gasps. It was a wet sound, as if the air was turning to liquid and drowning was inevitable. I needed to try the door to the outside again. I needed to get my neighbor's attention. I needed to escape. But my primal instincts had kicked in—the ones that operate just below the surface, electric and almost imperceptible, and they kept me frozen in place. Like a deer in the forest, alert and impossibly still.

Someone was in the other room.

The prewar wooden floors that I didn't have the energy to drape with rugs amplified sound. On the rare occasions that I had worn high heels on my way out, my head would throb with the sharp staccato sound of each step as it stabbed the wood and reverberated against the tall ceiling. And it was that very sound I heard, echoing through the brittle surfaces of my apartment, taking measured steps. Coming closer.

Clack. Clack. Clack.

I stayed still.

Clack. Clack. Clack.

The sound was coming down the hallway between the apartment door and bedroom door. There was something else. A glow. A wavering, unreliable aura made its way through the dark apartment. Candlelight. The kind of light that I had previously found comforting in its particular shape, color, and warmth. Candlelight meant safety during power outages, intimacy during dinners, and commitment during a wedding. But now the brightness morphed into something sinister.

The sound of footsteps grew louder. The candlelight grew brighter. My nervous system and skeletal system and muscles turned to cement. I was hardened in fear. When the sound and light finally filled the doorway, my breath stopped altogether, and my bedroom became a vacuum—void of air and life and safety.

The woman in the red dress was holding the candle I had lit during the Three Kings Game. Her dress was the color of that particular kind of blood that pours from deep within the body—the almost black shade of mortal peril. Her face was a chalky white, and it cracked and flaked like a dry desert bed. Like something long dead. Her lips were painted in the shape of a red heart, slightly smudged and smeared as if it had been made of blood. She was exactly what my brain would have conjured if I had tasked it with imagining the most terrifying version of the Queen of Hearts. It didn't occur to me just then that perhaps that's exactly what she was.

She began speaking to me, and her words and breath made the candle flame in her hands flicker erratically. I couldn't register what she was saying—her words flowed over and through me as terror melted my brain, and it sloshed helplessly inside of my skull.

As she spoke, my melted brain started to bubble and boil and scald the inside of my body. By the time she walked from the doorway to the side of my bed, I was a frozen shape, sculpted by intense fright, and when I reached into what was left of my survival instincts to produce a scream, nothing was there. I had been completely hollowed out. All traces of my humanness had been melted by the feelings she had caused me to feel. One final, rational thought flashed: there was a reason why the ritual called for the physical presence of another person. When people were together in the same place, the spirits could still scare them—like they had the weak-minded YouTubers, almost to death – but they could not harm them. Not really. I had done the ritual alone. In my solitude, The Queen had found a way in. That realization lingered for a moment before leaving behind a slimy trail of hopelessness. And then, there was nothing.

I could hear banging at my apartment door, and the buzzer rang repeatedly. The noise was distorted as if it was traveling underwater, but I could tell it was Joe's voice.

"Beth! Beth! Open the door!"

Another figure, which could have only been The Fool, appeared next to The Queen. He was dressed in a black harlequin outfit – not unlike the one from my ugly poster – with a cracked white face – similar to The Queen's. He had a black spade painted over one eye and was holding something in his hand. A scepter? His grin was thin and oddly shaped, like a child's clumsy drawing.

The Queen's eyes were like dark sapphires in the candlelight, flashing wildly and with a sinister gleam. I couldn't pull myself from them. I couldn't think or move. I was an empty vessel.

No. She had made me into *her* vessel.

"Beth! Answer the door or I'm calling the cops! Beth!" There was Joe. My surprising knight in shining armor. I tensed up, bristling at the thought that he might have been too late.

In one breath, The Queen extinguished the candle, and, somehow, my laptop. Everything was dark, but I could still feel her standing over me. As she bent over me, I could smell her acrid breath, like roses that had been left to rot in the vase a little too long, and she covered me like a blanket, seeping into my skin. And then, her arms became my arms. Her face became my face. And her rage became my rage. The Fool giggled next to us.

"Beth! I'm not leaving. Open the door!"

Beth was gone. I inhabited her skin and bones and greasy hair, but nothing else was left of her. It was only me. The Queen. And I needed to get back inside the mirror.

"Beth!"

Everything outside of the mirror was sharp and jarring. I needed to get back to where everything was smooth and dreamlike. Where pain and anger thrived instead of destroyed. Where there are no sharp edges or boundaries, and where the world is reflected back in its flawed reality. There is no hiding from a reflection, after all. The Fool had helped me sniff out loneliness and find a vulnerable King in Beth. It had been easy to invade her. To dissolve her until nothing was left except her malleable flesh.

"Beth! Beth! Open the door!"

I pulled the door open. The man standing there was panicked—his eyes filled with deep concern and an intimate kind of caring that I quickly realized had gone wholly unnoticed by Beth. Shame. He saw Beth's face and heard Beth's voice reassure him that everything was fine. He didn't seem satisfied and he asked to come inside. I laughed and waved him off before closing the door.

The Fool appeared in front of me, grinning. He was like an almost joyful Grim Reaper, with his comedic scepter topped with a jingle bell—his version of the Reaper's scythe that he rings when the game has been won and the King has been conquered.

There was one last thing left to do.

I found the shard of glass in the corner of the living room that Beth had carelessly left when I had made the mirror fall off the chair, causing it to break. It was small but sharp. It would do.

I could hear the voices from The Shadowside begin to fill the apartment with whispers, popping and hissing like a pot beginning to boil, transforming its contents into something new. The Fool's bell had not yet rung. I had subdued the King but not yet won.

I dragged the glass along Beth's left arm from wrist to elbow, and then did the same to her right arm, watching as the serpentine streams of blood wriggled out of her.

I curled up on the floor, placing Beth's hands underneath her head like illustrations of demure sleeping princesses I had seen. The blood pooled under her head like a velvet pillow, fit for royalty. Humans are so terribly weak. So seduced by the idea of crafting a satisfying reflection that they will do anything. The voices from The Shadowside grew louder and more urgent. The Fool laughed. *Death is only temporary*, he hissed. *Just like life.*

The last thing I would hear in Beth's frail human ears was the ringing of The Fool's jingle bell. The sound of victory. Of conquest. A sound that meant I was free to slip back into the mirror. There was one left in Beth's apartment. A small one in the bathroom. I gave Beth a final glance. Though people would certainly mourn her, no one would be surprised by her self-inflicted death. Shame.

Here in the mirror—in The Shadowside—is

where I lurk. Sliding and drifting behind peoples' reflections. Behind the imperfect images that people are often afraid to see when they look at themselves. Here is where I wait for another King.

The Closet Game

I live in a haunted house. This fact would unsettle most people. I, however, loved it. Our house is what you would expect a haunted house to look like: large, sprawling, and situated on the top of a hill overlooking a bucolic town below.

There are several entities that live in our house. There's a kind older woman who checks on me at night and rubs my hair with an invisible hand. There's a mischievous one that hides my homework in cereal boxes and my shoes in the dryer. There's the Screaming Woman, who, as her name suggests, screams in the basement and walks around the backyard at night, just out of reach of the bright perimeter of the security floodlights. And then there was the one that I conjured while playing a game.

It had been my idea to gather my friends in the vending machine room at school on Halloween to tell ghost stories. Since ghosts were a part of my daily life at home, the more I encountered them, the more my fear of them was transformed into a fascination and even a healthy respect. On this holiday of spirits, I found myself jonesing for a ghost fix at school. Somehow word of this idea spread, and the storytelling had evolved from three of my closest friends to thirteen people with a similar fright addiction (and free period). This was going to be fun.

We unplugged the machines, closed the door, and turned out the lights. One by one, we started sharing stories. Sometimes they were firsthand, other times they had happened to a best friend's-cousin's-neighbor. There we were, bonded together in darkness, enjoying the simultaneous feeling of safety in numbers and fear.

Then it was Jake's turn. When I heard his voice from the other side of the room, I was grateful he couldn't see me rolling my eyes in the dark. Jake was, to put it delicately, kind of a jerk. My fervent dislike of him could be traced back to English class freshman year when he critiqued a poem I had written so cruelly that it made me cry. I settled in and prepared myself for his self-indulgent drivel.

"Have you guys ever heard of the closet game?"

A murmur of "no's" rippled through the room.

"Ok. So, my friend Liam heard about it from another friend of his and decided, stupidly, to play it."

I shook my head. Liam. Jake liked to spread rumors and make up stories (for instance, during sophomore year he made up a story about me making out with the King of the Nerds), and I could already tell he was making up this story. Even the name of his main character was heavy-handed.

"In the closet game, you wait until dark, take a book of matches into your bedroom, and turn off all the lights. You have to have a walk-in closet—which Liam does because he's a rich a-hole—that you can close yourself inside of. Then, you say some hocus pocus and wait."

He allowed room for a dramatic pause. After a few moments, a voice piped up: "What…happens next?"

"Well, I guess you hear whispering, and then you light the match. If you don't light it right away, something grabs you from behind and drags you into eternal darkness."

"Let me guess. Liam was dragged into eternal darkness and you never saw him again?" I retorted drily. I couldn't help myself. The darkness had given me bravado, and I had grown tired of hearing Jake's voice.

"Shut up, Harper." A chorus of "oooos" and a whispered "sick burn, Jake" followed. I rolled my eyes again.

He continued. "So, anyway, after you light the match, you have to leave the closet and close the door without looking behind you. If you play the game right, you can never look in your closet in the dark again. If you do, you'll see two glowing red eyes, watching you."

He let the room fall silent again so that the suspense could build. "And Liam played this game. And he…." Jake's voice broke. He choked on sobs, which was completely unlike him. The person sitting next to me in the dark gripped my hand. I was pretty sure Jake was faking it. Maybe. Nevertheless, a feeling of dread roiled in my gut.

"What happened to Liam?" A nervous voice asked.

Jake started bawling. There was a collective intake of breath.

"You guys…the game is real. And Liam…" more sobbing. "Nothing happened to Liam." Jake's voice was instantly deadpan. "He lived happily ever after."

He got what he wanted: a strong reaction from everyone. We almost missed hearing the bell over the sound of voices groaning, cursing, and even laughing. Someone flipped on the light switch, and we all blinked under the unforgiving fluorescent bulbs. I glared at Jake as we exited the room, and he responded with a sneer. Some people had no respect for ghost stories.

Three nights later, on a Friday, I found myself in a position that I hadn't experienced in over a year: dateless. My boyfriend, Trey, was sidelined with dry sockets after having his wisdom teeth removed, and was in quite a bit of pain. I felt slightly responsible, as apparently making out is frowned upon after oral surgery, but we couldn't quite help ourselves. At six-foot-two, he was a full foot taller than me, and his limbs and features were lanky and awkward, almost as if he had yet to grow into him—although I couldn't imagine it would be possible for him to grow much more. He kept his brown hair longer on top and shaved underneath, and it was always a little greasy and unkempt. Set in that long thin face was a pair of remarkable cornflower blue eyes. We had blue eyes in common, but our physical similarities ended there. I was built compact and athletic, and my blonde hair was several inches longer and several shades lighter than his. Missing a Friday night date was a dramatic, tantrum-inducing event because we went to different schools and rarely saw each other during the week.

I was home alone—apparently, everyone else in my family had an actual social life, and my parents had no worries about leaving me home alone because they knew I didn't that night—and curled up in the corduroy armchair in the TV room, releasing ballooning sighs of boredom to no one in particular. I had already watched several episodes of *America's Next Top Model* and texted Trey until his painkillers kicked in and he fell asleep. I decided to call the one person with whom I still spoke on the phone instead of texting: my best friend Rue.

Rue and I met two summers earlier during a miserable summer job at an overly air-conditioned movie theater—the same summer job where I met Trey. Both Rue and Trey lived almost an hour from me, out in the country, and that summer they made the long haul to work every day. The three of us went to different schools and a little variety in socializing felt great for all of us. For Trey and me it was, as they say, love at first sight (or, if I'm honest, total lust at first sight) and Rue settled into the role of third wheel a bit reluctantly. Rue and I had completely opposite personalities: she was the shy, awkward introvert to my ebullient extrovert. She was mousy with freckles and a penchant for Wal-Mart jeans, and I preferred J.Crew and ribbon belts. She attended a Lutheran high school and lived with a devoutly Christian mother, which was a stark contrast to my preppy private school and atheist parents. But, as rigid as our parents were in their respective values, we were flexible. The particular common ground of the boring summer job, combined with our immersion in social media, seemed to have given both of us an open mind. We grew to not only accept but love each other, and I thought she was the most hilarious person I knew—if a bit of a nerd who was quite comfortable in her safety zone of rule-following. In a short amount of time, we developed a solid kind of intimacy that kept me moored when things got stormy at school. Communicating over the phone with our voices instead of texts had been her ground rule, because, as she put it, texting would "cheapen our bond."

Since Rue lacked any semblance of a social life, I figured she was curled up in a similar position on a similar armchair and preparing herself for the Friday night ritual that she looked forward to all week: a marathon of trashy TV. After all, it was the one night her mother's TV ban was lifted.

As it turned out, she was getting ready for a date.

I sprang to my feet in incredulous shock. "WHAT?! And you're just telling me about this NOW??"

"Well, I don't want to jinx anything." her voice was sheepish in a way that I had never heard before, followed by a truly surprising sound: the trill of a girlish giggle. "I mean, if I told you, I was afraid I'd come down with laryngitis or chickenpox."

My mouth was still dangling open. I closed it and collected myself.

"Y'know, that's an awfully superstitious way to think for a church-going girl. Also, you've already *had* chickenpox."

This was, by all accounts, Rue's first date. And not just any date. She was going out with the cutest guy in her high school. JD. He had seen the bumper sticker on her car—the one from her favorite coffee/ice cream shop, Frost and Steam—and asked if she wanted to get a cappuccino with him that night. As one of only five students in school who owned a car, she would, of course, drive.

Even I had to admit he was cute. He had played Joseph in their perilously under-budgeted version of *Joseph and the Technicolor Dreamcoat*, which Rue had dragged me to see. She was so transfixed the entire time that I had to check her pulse once or twice. After the show, though, I realized the extent of her competition, as he was swarmed by a giggling, saving-ourselves-for-marriage crowd of girls.

I cradled the phone against my shoulder as I opened a can and dumped the contents into a pot on the stove. Dinner of champions. "So I guess this means you don't want to come over for some tomato soup and video games?"

"You know I love you, and that's tempting. But, no."

"Bummer."

"Well, it IS a crime that Trey is leaving you unattended on a Friday. Maybe you should dump him and conjure up a ghost date tonight. And then you and I and your ghost date can all go out and you guys can make me dry heave at the movies, and at dinner, and at the car wash…"

Touché. Even I could admit that Trey and I were overly-effusive with the public displays of affection.

I couldn't help but release a labored moan as a

guilt trip. It wasn't fair, but I did it anyway.

"I'm sorry," Rue said, distractedly. I could tell her apology was less than genuine. I think she was too busy curling her bangs.

"It's ok," I said, imitating the passive-aggressive tone my mother frequently used. "Well, don't kiss him on the first date or else Satan will drag your soul to hell, or whatever religious crap your mom always says."

She chuckled and then paused. "Hey....be careful tonight."

"What do you mean? I'm the one staying home!" I exclaimed.

"I know. But I just got a weird feeling all of a sudden. Are you sure you're gonna be ok? Maybe I *should* come over...." I could tell that Rue was getting nervous about her date because her voice was climbing higher in pitch.

I had to stop myself from telling her to come over. I took a deep breath and decided to be the bigger person. "Oh, no way am I going to interrupt your hot date! Besides, I have a fresh series of *Women Who Kill* waiting for me to binge-watch."

"Ugh. You and that series," she groaned. I could hear the click of the curling iron as she put the phone on speaker. "So, you're sure you're ok? You'll be careful?"

"Uh, *you're* the one who needs to be careful," I retorted. "By the way, I put two Trojans in your glove box."

"Oh, Holy Hannah, Harper." This was the closest she ever got to a curse. I bellowed a laugh, and it traveled from the TV room, into the hallway, and echoed against the high ceilings of the house. I stopped laughing. I could hear that the noise hadn't bounced against any living, breathing, 98.6-degree people. It was a blatant reminder that I was home alone.

"Hey, have fun tonight and enjoy your time with JD. Call me with the details tomorrow, ok?"

"Absolutely. And call me if you need me."

We hung up, and I ate my canned soup in front of the TV. I was starting to feel sorry for myself when I remembered something important: being home alone meant that I could sneak a cigarette without getting caught by my parents. Smoking was my dirty little secret that I kept hidden from Trey and Rue. It was the sole reason I was grateful that we went to different schools because smoking just beyond the school property boundary was a favorite pastime for my classmates and me.

I grabbed my cigarettes, put on the smoking hat and jacket that I used to prevent the smell of smoke from soaking into my hair and clothes, and headed through the kitchen to the sliding glass door that led to the backyard. I sat on the steps, lit my cigarette, and took a deliciously long drag. Spring had rushed in and began its busy work of melting the snow and ordering things to grow. The crabapple tree a few feet away was starting to lose its flowers. It seemed to only be in full bloom for a few days. Just beyond it, my mother's gardens lined a long retaining wall, and even in the dark, I could sense them pushing their way through the earth. Everything was coming alive again.

Spring also meant that the ghosts in our house

would begin to grow dormant. They were mostly active and occasionally troublesome during the fall and winter months. It was during those months that some of my friends, especially Rue, would avoid my house. Our gatherings were often interrupted by ghostly footsteps, doors opening and closing on their own, and the occasional disembodied voice. I enjoyed watching my friends' scared reactions. Trey always tried to find a logical and scientific explanation for everything. He found my belief in ghosts "adorable," and because he did not share it, he was unfazed when strange things did happen. One time he did see the Woman in White drifting through my snowy back yard, leaving no trace of footprints, and into the forest. He blamed a trespassing teenager with a penchant for vintage clothing and a strong wind that dissolved all evidence of her trail.

Right.

I had to admit that I missed the ghosts when they were quiet. Their presence excited me, and, when Trey was around, the adrenaline rush they provided sent me leaping into his arms.

I ashed my cigarette and picked up my phone. Trey hadn't responded to my good night text, so I knew he was asleep. I thumbed through my contacts. All of my closest friends—and, for that matter, acquaintances—had significant others, which meant that no one was home.

"You're all busy getting busy, I guess…" I muttered.

I set my phone down and lit another cigarette. As my eyes drifted to the sky and the insects began revving up, a strange feeling spread from my spine and out to my extremities. It was new and unusual. It took me a moment to realize that it was both boredom and loneliness.

"Maybe I *should* conjure a spirit." I knew Rue had been kidding when she made that suggestion. Her religious mother had instructed her that ghosts were manifestations of the Devil and should be avoided. *Whatever*. After sitting with this strange feeling for a few more minutes, I decided that I could either watch a horror movie or create my own.

I crushed my cigarette, walked back through the sliding glass door, and peeled off my smoky layer of clothes before throwing them in the washing machine. I grabbed a diet soda and climbed the creaky back staircase—they had been the servants' stairs long ago—to my bedroom. This night needed some incense, some old school Nirvana, and a ghost.

After preparing the first two, I sat at my desk, woke up my computer, and Googled how to communicate with spirits. "Let's see…The Bathtub Game…Three Kings Game…hide and seek with a doll…." Everything either seemed too far-fetched and complicated or required materials that I didn't have—such as another player. Something eventually caught my eye. "Hmmm. The Closet Game….'summon a demon to scare an enemy.' So I guess Jake wasn't creative enough to make that game up after all."

Like the other games I had browsed, this one came with the standard, all caps warning—DO

NOT PLAY THIS GAME—as well as incredibly specific rules and directions.

"Hmm. If no one should actually play any of these games, why provide such specific instructions?" As there was no one around to enjoy my wit, I turned to the teddy bear on my bed. "Amiright?"

He didn't answer.

"Alrighty. 'Step one: find a book of matches and wait until dark. This game won't work in the daylight. Step two: turn off all the lights, step inside the closet, and close the door.' Well. I guess only people with walk-in closets deserve to summon demons." I looked at my bedroom closet. It was long, but certainly not a walk-in. I would have to find another place to play the game. "'Step three: stand in the dark for two minutes, facing the closet door. Step four: take an unlit match, hold it in front of you, and say, *show me the light or leave me in darkness.* You will have summoned a demon. Say the name of the person you want to send the demon to three times. Each time that person looks inside of his or her closet, two glowing red eyes will be watching." I briefly skimmed the rest of the rules. If you hear whispering, light the match right away. Do not turn around. Something terrible will be lurking behind you. If you don't light the match fast enough, the thing behind you will drag you into eternal darkness.

"Wow. Dramatic, much? Eternal darkness? Really?" I took a sip of soda. This version of the game was an interesting variation from the one Jake had described. I liked the idea of sending a demon to scare someone. This was way better than the crank calls that my parents used to do when they were kids. I kept reading. The last few words of the instructions were written in bold letters. "IMPORTANT: Before leaving the closet, say aloud three times: 'Let no harm come to this person. Only fear.' If you fail to do this, there's no telling what the demon will do."

I shut my laptop. I knew the exact person that I wanted to scare. This was going to be fun.

I grabbed my lucky purple lighter and walked around the house, looking for the right closet to use for the game. Our house had been built 100 years earlier as a wedding gift for one of the founding families of our Minnesota town. According to the town records—the studying of which was a nerdy indulgence of mine that I did not advertise—they had earned their fortune by using the labor of indentured servants to harvest the ginseng root that had grown abundantly by the shores of Lake Minnetonka. This house had accommodated a mixture of souls, both wealthy and poor, and their energies mingled eternally within its walls.

The house was long and narrow, and on the upper level, a thin hallway snaked through it like a maze, lined with what seemed like endless doors. I checked the game closet, the cedar closet, and numerous linen closets, and none of them seemed quite right. After thinking for a few minutes, I realized that I had just the thing. It wasn't exactly a closet, but it would be perfect.

I returned to my bedroom, took a mental snapshot of the game instructions from my computer screen, grabbed my phone from where it was charging, and headed downstairs to the basement door.

All basements are creepy. They're damp, dark, and full of crawling things and forgotten objects. My basement, however, was the Vincent Price of basements. Much like the rest of the house, it was big and sprawling and filled with numerous rooms of different sizes and varying purposes. There was an old coal storage room with a doorway half the height of a normal door, and every once in a while, I would see a figure crouching inside with a grime-blackened face, shoveling coal that is no longer there. There was another space that had been converted into an amateur darkroom for developing photos, and another with a rectangular hole in the floor that had been haphazardly covered with bricks, almost as if something had been buried there. The stench of decades' worth of mouse carcasses decaying within the walls always hit me in the back of the throat as I descended the basement stairs. I only went down there during the spring and summer months, and only when it was absolutely necessary. During the fall and winter, the entities that dwelled there were busy and aggressive in a way that was more annoying than anything else. They would make all kinds of noise, and in a desperate bid for attention, one of them would constantly walk up and down the stairs. The sound of it would echo throughout the house.

The most notable tenant of the basement was The Screaming Woman. During the winter months, her screams would echo up through the vents and into my bedroom. Since my bedroom was at the opposite end of the house from everyone else's, I was the only one who heard her. When I first heard her screams at the age of nine, I was terrified. I would hide under the covers all night, squeezing my stuffed bunny and pulling a pillow over my head. My parents assured me that it was just steam from the radiators. When I finally mustered the bravery to venture down to the basement to explore, barefoot in my flannel nightgown, her screams transformed to a melodic humming. It was her way of telling me that she meant no harm. After that night, her screams lulled me to sleep. A strange lullaby, indeed.

I opened the door to the basement and, after making the decision to keep the lights off for a maximum adrenaline surge, turned on my phone's flashlight. Even in my socks, which wouldn't be white much longer, my footsteps thudded loudly on the hollow stairs. I made my way to the middle of the basement until I reached the perfect place for the closet game.

Having been previously owned by several generations of wealthy people before we moved in, the basement contained a floor-to-ceiling vault installed right in its dank center, for storing what I imagined to be numerous valuables. I thought of it as the house's stomach, and its presence was intimidating. It was also, as far as I was concerned, its best feature. After all, how many people lived in a house with a walk-in vault? I loved spooking my friends by taking them on basement tours, and I enjoyed the particular kind of affection I felt toward

Trey when I showed him the basement for the first time. Like I said, for me, the excitement of the supernatural motivated more...natural acts.

The vault was the first place where I met The Screaming Woman. One night many years ago, shortly after we had moved in, I had fallen asleep and my dream-self had wandered downstairs—still in my nightgown, but this time with bunny slippers—and the vault was illuminated by the eye-frying single bulb that hung from its ceiling. As my bunny feet shuffled closer, I saw someone inside of it. It was a woman—I could tell by the broad bell skirt—and she was moving things around, searching for something with a sense of urgency. Finally, she opened a box, made a small yet joyful sound, and retrieved a bundle of envelopes. They were tied together with a pale blue bow. I knew enough at the age of nine to be able to tell that they were her secrets. She held them to her chest and turned around, noticing me. And then, her mouth dropped open—further than any human jaw could manage—and from that gaping wet hole, an excruciating scream emanated. It was many pitches at once, like multiple voices mingling together into horrific tones, screaming out their pain and anger. The single bulb in the safe shattered, and I woke up.

I was fairly certain that the Screaming Woman had been in a great deal of pain and died tragically. Otherwise, why all the screaming? I was also certain that the vault had held something important to her. If I wanted to summon a demon, whatever energy was within the vault would most likely amplify the game. I stepped inside and set my phone on one of the empty shelves. It took two hands to heave the door mostly—but not all the way—shut. Even though the locking mechanisms in the door had long since rusted into immobility, I didn't want to run the risk of accidentally locking myself inside.

I picked up my phone and did a quick flashlight scan of the vault. There was nothing out of the ordinary—just a lot of dust and cobwebs. I pulled a lighter out of my pocket. Even though the instructions called for matches, I didn't want to take that particular gamble, because I was never able to light them on the first try. For this game, failing to light the match on the first try could lead to something more insidious than I was willing to take on at the moment. Then, I turned off my phone.

The pitch-black tended to evoke two reactions for me: stillness or panic. I find it to be either comforting or terrifying, depending on the circumstances. There in the vault, I let the stillness take over. It was so quiet – like being in a filthy womb. I almost didn't want to disturb this peculiar kind of peace. But, I can never leave something alone once I've begun it. And I was going to summon a demon tonight.

"Ok. Let's see if can do this right. '*Show me the light or leave me in darkness.*'" And then, I said the name of my target three times: "Jake Dwyer, Jake Dwyer, Jake Dwyer." I paused. Since I was already communicating with the supernatural, I decided to ad-lib. "Believe me. Jake deserves a good scare. Give him hell….no pun intended." I was feeling comfortable, and a bit cocky in my bravery, and so I figured I would push the envelope a little more. "Also, while I'm here, I would like to ask The Screaming Woman to join me here tonight. I think this vault was important to her because I've seen it in my dreams. And so, Screaming Woman, if you are listening, I would like to speak with you. Maybe I can, you know, help you." I heard nothing. I waited. After what seemed like a few minutes, I started to get restless. I thought there was a step I was forgetting, but I couldn't be entirely sure. In any case, it felt as though the game needed closure, but I wasn't quite sure what to say. "Ok. That's it." That felt good enough for me.

Something eventually started to happen. Whispers came from behind me. It sounded like one meek voice at first. And then it was joined by another voice. And then another, and then another. Their whispers were soft and low, but after a few minutes of intent listening, I could make out a few words here and there: "Daemonium dominae." "Exspiravit." "Imperium." I didn't know exactly what they were saying, but I had seen enough exorcism movies to know that they were speaking Latin.

A shiver vibrated through me. This was frightening and exhilarating, and a tangle of feelings knotted in my gut. Just as the fear was starting to win, I lit the lighter. The flame appeared on the first try, and the whispering stopped as if on command.

"Cool…" I murmured.

I pushed open the door of the vault, exited it, and turned back around. I blinked hard and rubbed my eyes. The vault was dark inside, but there, hovering and flickering slightly—almost like candle flames—were two glowing orbs. Eyes. *The game had actually worked.* They were a warm yellow, and I figured that since they were not red, they were not demon eyes. I didn't get an evil feeling from them, and so that could only mean one thing: they belonged to The Screaming Woman.

I watched them for a while, waiting to see if they would move or blink or do anything at all. But they just stayed there, glowing in place.

"Hi. I'm Harper. I'm guessing you're The Screaming Woman I've seen a few times since I invited you here. Um…I'd like to, you know, help you if I can. I think something bad happened to you. Can you just, like, tell me about it? If you want, I mean…."

Silence. I waited, but she wasn't talking.

"Ok. Well, I'm going upstairs to watch reality TV, but I'll check in on you tomorrow." I turned my flashlight back on and walked through the basement and up the stairs, leaving the door closed behind me. I smiled. My dateless Friday night hadn't been so boring after all.

I grabbed some cookies and milk, sank back into the armchair, and scrolled to my show. It didn't take long for me to doze off.

I was startled awake by a scream coming from the basement directly below me. I ran down to the basement, flipping on the lights as I went. There was no Screaming Woman, and when I looked into the vault, the eyes were gone.

"You guys. I need to tell you something crazy.

74

You'll never believe it!" I gestured emphatically and dropped my voice to a whisper. I had ushered a small group of intrigued classmates over to a corner of the common area after first period. When I could tell that all eyes were on me, I leaned forward, clasped my hands together, and mustered my best storytelling voice. "The closet game works!"

"What? Really?" My friend Joe's bespectacled eyes looked owlish in their curiosity. "Are you serious or are you messing with us like he did?" He gestured with his head over to Jake, who was within earshot.

"I'm dead serious. You guys, I played the closet game on Friday, and it was so scary. The craziest thing happened." I glanced over at Jake, who I could tell was pretending not to listen. My friends had a lot of follow-up questions, which we decided were best answered over a cigarette. We grabbed our coats and smokes, and I walked over to the table where Jake was sitting and leaned on my elbows. He kept his eyes glued to his Nietzsche. Of course he would be reading Nietzsche.

"So…did you see anything in your closet over the weekend? Other than your hideous collection of polyester shirts?" In that moment I had some degree of earnestness. I wanted to know if my experiment had worked.

"Go away, Harper." His eyes stayed on the page. I tried to read his body language for a moment. Surely if he had seen a demon in his closet, he would somehow give it away.

I shrugged and headed toward the door while he put on his headphones. For a moment, I felt a pang of guilt. Maybe sending a demon to someone's house wasn't the nicest thing to do. *Let it go, Harper. That guy is too pompous for his own good.* Besides, there was no evidence to suggest that I had succeeded in sending a demon anywhere.

I waited until dark that day to go back down to the basement and see if the eyes I had seen during the game were there. They were gone. Oh well. At least it had made for a good story and a brief moment in the spotlight.

It was difficult to stay within the speed limit as I drove to Trey's house the following Friday night. He was finally feeling better. His parents had taken his younger sister to a Taylor Swift concert and asked one of their neighbors to come over and chaperone us. "Neighbor" is perhaps a generous word, as his house was separated from Trey's by several acres of land, but still he was the closest person in the vicinity. The neighbor was a crotchety old man who had about as much interest in us as we did in him, and while he wanted to stay on Trey's parents' good side (after all, they watched over his property whenever he was gone), he wanted nothing to do with us. His chaperoning consisted of the same routine: at the beginning of the night, he would stop by, grunt, tell us not to burn the place down, and we would sneak him a few sips of Trey's father's favorite scotch. He would come back a few minutes before Trey's parents were expected home, grunt some more, and tell them we stayed out of trouble as soon as they walked in the door. We had several hours of alone time in front of us. And I knew just how to use them.

Trey answered the door in his usual at-home outfit: plaid flannel shirt, faded jeans, and sheepskin slippers. He was snuggly and sexy at the same time, and I couldn't wait to throw my arms around him.

Without a word, he picked me up and carried me to his bedroom. He had strung fairy lights over the windows and lit candles, and I was grateful that his early 90s band posters and weird collection of dragon figurines were obscured. I was overwhelmed by how badly I wanted him.

He laid me on his bed—it was made, for once—and whispered into my ear, "I missed you so much." I told him I had missed him too, and then we proceeded to show each other just how much.

Later, we assumed our favorite position of spooning. Trey kissed the back of my neck several times before nestling his face there. Before I could relax fully, I needed to first flip my phone over and check the time. There was plenty of time for a nap before the rest of his family members and the grizzled neighbor were expected home.

After a few minutes, Trey was snoring softly behind me, and I needed a glass of water. I kissed his hand before wiggling out from under his arm, and, after throwing on his shirt that had been discarded on the floor, walked downstairs to the kitchen. I took advantage of being alone in his house and did some looking around. Trey's family seemed, to me, like a bunch of country bumpkins, but generations of successful horse breeding and a sense of frugality had made them wealthy. Not that you would know it to look at them. I looked at their many family photos and noticed Trey's father's go-to outfit was a Canadian tuxedo: a long-sleeved denim shirt paired with jeans. My mind drifted to what my family photos would look like with Trey, years from now. I pictured the kids with his blue eyes and my blonde hair. And probably dressed in flannel.

From upstairs came a thump. It was so loud I thought that Trey had fallen out of bed. But when I went back upstairs to check on him, he was in the exact same position as when I had left and snoring even more loudly than before. When I scanned the room, I saw that something had fallen out of his closet, leaving the door ajar. It was a *Dungeons and Dragons* tome the size of a small child, and he had obviously shoved it in there out of sight before I came over.

"Trey, you're such a dork," I whispered as I picked up the book and went to replace it on the shelf.

Inside the closet there were two glowing red eyes, watching me. I let out a startled half-scream and dropped the book.

"Harper?" Trey's voice had a coating of sleepiness over it.

"Uh, I saw a spider." I shoved the book back in the closet and closed the door. "Listen, we should get dressed and make it look like we've been playing cards all night before your parents get home."

"What's your preference? Hearts or Spades?"

I laughed and threw his shirt at him. When he went to the bathroom I looked in the closet again.

78

The eyes were gone. Maybe it was a trick of the light and they had never been there in the first place. Either way, they were nothing to worry about. *Thank goodness.*

The next morning, Saturday, I woke up to six missed calls and a series of all caps texts from Rue. She never texted me.

When I called her back, her voice was frantic. "What did you do?" she whisper-demanded.

"What do you mean?" I was taken aback.

"When I told you to conjure a spirit, did you *actually* conjure one?"

Her question was a punch in the gut, followed by a spreading feeling of panic. *Uh oh.*

"Um, why?" I tried to sound casual.

"Because there's something *in my closet.*" She hissed the words.

This was not good.

"Ok. Sit tight. I'm coming over."

I pulled open my laptop and found the game instructions again. I had sent the demon to Jake's closet—where it apparently didn't materialize, as far as I knew—not Rue's, and certainly not Trey's. And then I saw it: the last line of the game. The line that prevented the demon from doing any harm. I had completely omitted it when I did the summoning. And evidently, because I hadn't given the demon the rules, it wasn't obligated to stay in one place and do no harm. I clearly had a rogue demon on my hands. *This was **really** not good.*

I threw a sweatshirt and scarf on over my pajamas, yelled down the hall to my parents that I was going to Rue's, and headed out. My hands shook on the wheel as I drove. This should not be happening. "I mean, if I summoned a demon, I can unsummon it too…right?" I said to myself. It gave me a brief feeling of relief. But only for a minute. I was clearly out of my depth.

Rue had such a frightened and enraged look on her face when she opened the door that I was afraid she would spit on me. Wordlessly she dragged me by the wrist to her bedroom.

"Last night I heard squeaking coming from my closet. I thought it was a sick mouse, so I opened the door and there were RED EYES, Harper. Red. Eyes. But then…" Rue grabbed the tops of my arms and dug her nails in, making me wince, "…it spoke." Her eyes got wide and she shook me once for emphasis.

"What?? It spoke?" I didn't really want to know the answer to my next question, but I asked it anyway. "What did it say?"

"It said 'amicus falsus.' I never thought I'd be glad for the Latin classes my mom forced me to take, but I understood it."

"What…what does that mean?" I remembered the Latin whispers I had heard during the game. Whatever this entity was, it was the same one I had heard in the vault. But why was it here?

"It means 'false friend.' *A demon in my closet just growled 'false friend' at me.* I'm sorry I didn't hang out with you last weekend, but if you sent a…*fucking*…demon to my closet…" She was cursing under her breath so that her parents wouldn't hear. She never cursed. Her nails dug deeper into my arms, and I shook her off.

"Stop. No, I didn't send you a demon. Geez, why would you ever think that? Calm down. Get ahold of yourself. You just whispered a swear word in your parents' house! You're out of control!" I thought about slapping her for dramatic effect, but she had turned away before I had the chance.

Rue walked to her bed and slumped down on it. She put her head in her hands and let out a low whine. I had no idea what was going on, and all I could think to do was sit next to her. "Then God is punishing me because I let JD get to second base." She laid back on her bed and covered her face with a pillow. "I'm sorry I thought it was you," she said with a muffled voice, "when it was my fault."

I wanted to know more about JD getting to second base—and I was briefly pissed that she had lied to me and said nothing had happened when I asked about her date—but that would all have to wait. I was distracted by an uncomfortable feeling bubbling in my stomach. Guilt. I pulled the pillow off of her.

"Ok, ok. Here's the thing. God isn't mad at you. I...might have summoned a demon." Rue sat up so abruptly that I was afraid she would hit me. I told her the details of what I had done, almost as if it was a confessional and she was my enraged priest. I steepled my fingers as if in prayer. "But I sent it to someone else! Not you! I don't know why that thing is in your closet, but I promise I didn't send it here. Also..." I really dreaded telling her this, "I think it might be in Trey's closet as well."

Rue's face was a flash of confusion and anger.

She started to speak, but then looked away.

"Also…." I was already in this deep. I might as well keep going. "I was supposed to say something at the end of the game to prevent the demon from doing any harm. But, well, I sort of…forgot."

"A game?! You saw this as a game?! And you FORGOT the MOST IMPORTANT PART?" I grabbed a pillow and placed it between us as a buffer. Rue stood up and paced back and forth for a few minutes. I pulled my legs under me as I sat on her bed and tried to will myself to disappear.

"You have really messed up. Do you know that? You have messed up. I know you think ghosts are fun or exciting or whatever, but God has burned cities for less. You can't just play around with the supernatural!"

She waited for me to respond, but I had nothing to say. It was difficult to defend myself against a vengeful God. She continued.

"And now you've put me AND Trey in danger. I don't know why that thing was in our closets. It makes no sense. But you know what? Nothing demons do make sense! Do you know why? Because they're evil! Which is why you aren't supposed to – *fuck* – with them! And not only did you summon one, but you *forgot* to tell it not to do any harm? And who the hell knows—maybe it wouldn't have listened anyway. Do you know why? Because it's EVIL! I *just can't* with you right now." Rue began changing her clothes, digging through drawers, and running around her house. She darted upstairs, and as I listened to her footsteps crisscrossing the floor above me, I decided it was

82

best to stay put. She was scaring me. I had never seen her like this and had no idea that she had this kind of rage in her. When she returned to her bedroom, she was wearing an army green waffle-knit shirt, had a messenger bag slung across her body, her favorite pair of hideous combat boots were on, and she wore a determined facial expression that was completely unfamiliar to me. My mind flashed to Sigourney Weaver in Aliens. In that moment, I would've taken my chances with the demon.

"Let's go," she growled. I nodded and complied. She didn't speak to me as she drove us to Trey's house.

Trey's mother had plump, pleasant features and a face peppered in freckles, which masked a severe and emotionally detached personality. As she answered the door, I cowered behind Rue.

"Well, hello, girls! Are we expecting you?" Trey's mother looked from Rue, to me, to Rue again, her eyes narrowing slightly.

"Hi, Mrs. Baxter. Is Trey home? We have an urgent algebra question, and he is the person to answer it!" I recoiled slightly and looked at Rue, surprised. She usually spoke in a low, respectful tone and avoided eye contact when forced into conversation with adults. I was also impressed that she seemed to know that the way to Mrs. Baxter's heart was to compliment her son's impressive brainpower.

Mrs. Baxter smiled, but only for a second. "Well, Trey might be under the weather. Usually, he's up at 6 to help us with the horses, but I couldn't wake him up today. I think he needs his rest. He's still asleep right now."

I looked at my watch. It was 12:00 p.m. Trey never slept this late. Something was wrong.

I gave Rue a nudge. "Oh, that lazy bones," she said, putting a hand on Mrs. Baxter's shoulder, "we'll get him out of bed. He's just avoiding his homework."

"I don't think he's up for company—"

Rue pushed past Mrs. Baxter and ran up the stairs to Trey's bedroom. I followed with my head bowed, willing her to not notice I was even there.

"You didn't even have time to get out of your pajamas? Wow. This really must be some algebra emergency," she shouted up the stairs after me. I pretended not to hear her.

Rue threw open Trey's door without knocking and locked it behind us. Before I had time to react, she was straddling him and pulling something out of her bag.

"What the hell, Rue?!" Seeing my best friend astride my boyfriend was not a sight I ever wanted to see, except in that awful nightmare I had that one time about the two of them. Sheesh.

"Shh!" She pulled open a small clear bottle and poured some of its contents into his mouth. He sputtered and sat up as Rue jumped off of him. We both backed away, as if he was an unpredictable wild animal, and waited for him to speak.

"Rue? Harps? What are you guys doing here?" He was disoriented, groggy, breathing unevenly. "Whoa. I was just having this crazy dream…there was this thing holding me down, and all I could see were its eyes…"

"Were they red?" Rue asked, shooting me a look.

"Yeah…how did you know that?"

"Your girlfriend seems to have summoned a demon and now for some reason, it's after both of us," Rue said as casually as if she was reporting the weather.

"Whaaa….?" Trey looked from Rue, to me, and back to Rue again. He rubbed his eyes vigorously and then looked at us again. I think he thought he was still asleep.

We heard the doorknob jiggle, followed by a knock. "Are you guys ok in there? Trey, are you alright? I told them to let you sleep."

Rue glared at Trey for a moment and whispered instructions in his ear.

"We're fine, mom! They just…need homework help. You can go back downstairs." We waited. Finally, her footsteps retreated. Once again, Trey rubbed his eyes and looked back and forth between us. "What the *hell* is wrong with you guys? Are you *high*?"

"Get dressed. We need to leave. Now." Rue ordered before turning on her heel and walking out of the room.

"Harps? What's going on? Where are we going?" Trey was dutifully throwing on his clothes. I noticed for a second that he hid behind them as if he suddenly didn't want me to see his body in a state of undress.

"I'm sorry," I whispered before leaving the room to let him finish getting dressed. I had barely spoken since we got to Trey's house. Part of my silence was shame and part of it was shock. I couldn't wrap my mind around what was happening—this crazy chain of events that I had put into motion. And who was this person who looked like Rue but acted nothing like her?

Trey was delayed by Mrs. Baxter, who insisted on taking his temperature. When he finally met us in Rue's car—she had reserved shotgun for him and I was banished to the back seat—he seemed spacey and out of it. Rue started barreling her station wagon down the road. "Tell him," she spat while eyeing me in the rearview mirror. And so I did. I gave him the full story of the closet game and everything that had happened since.

"But Rue, I have some questions." I leaned tentatively on the console between Rue and Trey, afraid for a moment that she would give me a backhanded slap from the driver's seat. She didn't, and so I proceeded. "Rue, you seem to have some experience with this kind of thing…"

Rue once again glared at me in the rearview mirror, shook her head, and then finally spoke. "I've never told you this, but my mom used to mess around with this kind of stuff. She had Ouija Boards and practiced a new-age form of witchcraft, and she would…summon things."

"Your mom? Your Bible-banging, Jesus-jazzing mother?"

"I know. It's hard to believe. It was a really crazy phase. So anyway, for a short time there was this clown entity with black eyes that would follow me around, and sometimes at night I would wake up and see it standing over my bed. My mom said that she had summoned a playful spirit to watch over me and that I shouldn't be afraid, but I knew it was evil. Its eyes were...so black. Then one night my mom had a dream that she was abducted by aliens. When she woke up she had a triangular bruise on her neck, which I guess is a mark that aliens will leave on someone they've abducted."

"What...the...hell...?" She might as well have been speaking an entirely different language. I couldn't comprehend what she was saying. I could tell Trey couldn't either because I saw him pinch himself to triple-check that he wasn't still asleep.

"Anyway, after that happened, she realized that she was playing with dangerous stuff. She accepted Jesus Christ as her Lord and Savior, got baptized, and never looked back."

This was a lot to process. Trey still seemed out of it. He stared out the window, but I didn't think he was really seeing anything.

"My mom did teach me how to get rid of the clown," Rue continued, "and I'm going to try the same thing today. But we have to do it where the demon was originally summoned."

"I cannot believe we are even having this conversation." I put my head in my hands. "I mean, I think my head might explode. You don't even like watching horror movies!"

"I hate this stuff!" She slapped the steering wheel. "I didn't ask for it! But for some reason, the crazy women in my life keep bringing it to me!" She was yelling. She never yelled.

I leaned back and crossed my arms, thinking.

We rode along in silence. I don't think Trey blinked once, and his jaw just kind of hung open.

I grappled with my perception of Rue's mother, and of Rue herself. I didn't know quite what to think. My parents were always busy with their own lives, on the opposite end of the house from where my bedroom was. We were not the kind of family that ate dinner together, or really spent much time together at all. Maybe that was part of why I liked Trey and Rue so much: their mothers were complicated, imperfect, and even a little intimidating, but they were present in a way that mine was not. Even Rue's mother, for all of her mistakes, still provided guidance and a way for Rue to find her way through something scary.

"Hey, Rue?" My voice squeaked, as I was a little afraid of her in that moment, "May I ask another question?"

She glared at me again in the rearview mirror but nodded.

"Why did I see white eyes and you saw red ones?"

Rue shrugged. "I've been thinking about that, and I'm not completely sure. You told me that when you were playing the game—and it's not exactly a game, *in case you haven't noticed*—you summoned the Screaming Woman, right? Well, it's possible that she was protecting you and blocking the demon. Think about it. Sure, the ghosts in your house are annoying at times, but nothing there actually wants to hurt you. Trey and I, though, aren't … 'lucky' enough to have ghosts protecting us."

I looked out the window, wiggling in my seat in an attempt to escape the uncomfortable things I was feeling. It was like my skin was being peeled from me in strips. I felt shame and fear – a leaden, bone-breaking, heavy kind of fear. I had opened a door that should have never been opened. This was real and dangerous. Rue was right: it wasn't just a game.

I looked back and forth between Trey and Rue—the people whom I loved more than anything. There was so much to lose. In that moment there was only one thing that would bring me any kind of relief. I pulled a cigarette out of my purse and lit it. I waited for Trey to whirl around with a look of disgust and surprise, and even scold me, but he was still too out of it. He just stared out the window.

Rue presented me with an open palm. "You got another one of those?"

Normally I would have passed out from shock to learn that Rue was also a secret smoker. But just then, nothing seemed shocking. As I handed her a cigarette, I realized that I didn't know my best friend at all. It was as if I had never really seen her—just the version of her that I needed to see. The version that I thought was reality. Except it wasn't. What else had I missed?

When we got to my house, my parents and sister were dispersed in their own areas. No one noticed we were there, and I was fairly confident that no one noticed I had been gone at all.

The three of us hurried down the basement stairs to the vault. Rue started barking orders like a lieutenant.

"Trey, hold this Bible firmly with both hands.

Harps, push the vault door open as far as it can go and close all the doors to the other rooms. We don't want this thing escaping and hiding somewhere else in the basement." I felt an enormous amount of trust in Rue as I ran around the basement shutting doors. I looked at Trey. He still hadn't said anything, and dutifully clutched the Bible with both hands. He was shaking a little.

"Stand behind me." Rue handed me a large wooden cross. It looked old, and I thought perhaps performing exorcisms was a talent that ran in her family over many generations. "No matter what happens, I need both of you to stay behind me. No matter how scared you are, *do not* run away." She had a clear bottle in her hand—the one she had used to rouse Trey—and I realized then that it was holy water. She turned her back to us, facing the vault, and put a silk purple scarf over her shoulders, which was embroidered with crosses. The vault was impossibly dark, even though the main basement lights were on. The darkness within it seemed almost alive. With an arc of her arm, Rue sent a smattering of holy water into it.

"Adiuro vos in nominee Iesu."

What. The. Hell. Now Rue was speaking Latin? And then, as though she had read my mind, she repeated the phrase in English: "I bind you in the name of Jesus Christ!" More holy water.

We stood still, waiting for something. And then, the red eyes appeared in the dark vault. Unblinking, glowing round and wide open like the retinas of a nocturnal animal in headlights. Animals seemed so far away and innocuous in that moment.

Rue threw the holy water again and repeated the Latin phrase.

"Adiuro vos in nominee Iesu. Leave this place!"

The basement was silent, and our breath and energy seemed to send strange vibrations through the air. It was as if we didn't belong. As if we were invading something else's rightful space. Then, a groan emanated from beneath us. As we stood there, a small lump formed, impossibly, in the cement floor, like a rat underneath a bedsheet. It started moving. Circling us. And then another lump formed. And another. And around and around they went.

"Rue, what are those?" I whispered. I could barely speak.

"I don't know," she snapped. She shifted her weight from one foot to the other, and I could tell that fear was beginning to agitate her. "It's like the demon has...tentacles or something. What did you do, Harps?"

"I...I don't know."

Rue repeated the Latin phrase and threw more holy water into the vault. The eyes remained unchanged, but the lumps in the floor – there were at least six of them – circled us even more quickly. I heard whimpering next to me and turned to look. Trey was crying and clutching the Bible to his chest. If I hadn't felt so scared myself, my empathy for him would have bowled me over. My hands were sweating as I held the cross. Rue kept repeating the banishing phrase, and the floor lumps grew larger and faster. Whatever she was doing, it wasn't working. I created this mess. I had to do something.

I held the cross above my head like a sword, took a deep breath, and found where my voice had been hiding deep inside of my abdomen. "I call upon the spirits of the house to help us. We need protection. Please help us." My voice was shaking so much I hardly recognized it. A growl emanated from within the vault. Rue backed up, and the three of us put our arms around each other. The growling continued and lumps in the floor grew taller and kept circling. Trey was openly weeping. We all clutched each other, not sure what to do next. The doors in the basement started swinging open and slamming shut by themselves, and the pipes began clanging as if something was hitting them. The floor trembled slightly.

"Please!" I yelled.

Then, the room filled with mist, and ghosts began to materialize.

"Oh my God—" Trey tried to dislodge himself and run away, but Rue's grip on him was surprisingly strong.

"No, no, no. It's ok. I promise. They're here to help," I said in my best imitation of a soothing voice that I could muster in that moment.

The ghosts became more solidified until they stood shoulder-to-shoulder behind us. The growling from the vault grew louder and started to form words.

"Mors vincit omnia…"

"What's it saying?" I whispered to Rue. A look of fear crumpled her face.

"Death conquers all," she whispered. Then she burst into tears. We wrapped our arms around each other more tightly.

I had summoned the spirits for protection, but it wasn't working. The voice in the vault continued growling and speaking in words I couldn't understand until they all blurred together in horrific syllables. The cement lumps grew until they were as tall as me and seemed to be forming arms as they circled around us, closing in. I shut my eyes. An assault of sound filled my ears. I felt something cold reach out and touch me.

And then, from behind me, I heard another voice:

"GET OUUUUUUUUT!" It was the Screaming Woman. All at once, the gathered ghosts began screaming. It was an otherworldly sound, so many pitches and volumes at once. Rue, Trey, and I unwrapped our arms from each other and covered our ears. One solitary, high-pitched squealing note rang out and then a column of black smoke burst forth from the vault, knocking us to the floor. The room was hazy and the musty air made us cough. As quickly as they had started, the noises stopped. When the smoke dispersed, the three of us were alone again. The ghosts were gone. After a few moments of catching our breath, Rue scrambled to her feet, looked in the dark vault, and ran throughout the basement searching the rooms. Trey and I stayed on the floor and embraced. I held him as his body shook with sobs.

"I'm sorry. I'm sorry…" I whispered into his ear. He pushed me away and wiped his eyes.

"I don't know what just happened. That was messed up. I need to get out of here."

Rue stood over both of us, her hands on her hips like a conquering hero. "Everything's gone. The ghosts, the demons everything." She looked down, meeting my gaze. It was as if a door in her head had shut, leaving her eyes as empty windows. "We are done here," she said.

I felt utterly stupid after everything I had put Rue and Trey through that day. But I was smart enough to know that she wasn't just talking about the exorcism.

She helped Trey to his feet and left me on the floor. "C'mon. I'm going to drive you home." She placed his arm over her shoulder and the two of them turned and walked up the basement stairs while I scrambled behind them. Rue made her way through the mudroom and out the back door without glancing back at me. Trey hovered for a moment at the door but kept his back to me. Something in him had retreated completely. It's remarkable how quickly things can change. I put my hand on his back.

"Trey…"

He forced himself to look at me, and I saw something frost over in those blue eyes. "I'll….I'll call you tomorrow. I gotta go." And with that, he slipped from my touch, out the door, and into Rue's car. I watched them drive away. I couldn't even chuckle as I usually did about her overly cautious use of the turn signal as she pulled out of my driveway and into the street. Devastation was forming in my body, but it was going to take a few days to reach my brain. At least I had time to prepare myself.

I walked to the TV room and sank into the corduroy chair. A minute later, my mom burst into the room

"Were you guys smoking in the basement? There's a smoky smell coming up through the vents!"

I could've told her the truth, but I knew she wouldn't believe me. She never believed me about the ghosts in the house. And if she ever had any encounters with them, she kept them to herself. I no longer cared if she found out about my dirty habit. I had nothing left to lose at that point. "Yes. Yes, we were. Or, well, I was."

She put both hands on her hips and clicked her tongue. "Well. You are most certainly grounded."

It didn't matter. Two months later, Trey and Rue still hadn't returned any of my calls, texts, or e-mails. I even drove to their houses, only to be turned away by their protective mothers, and the pang of so much longing for them would knock the breath out of me. My mom assured me that I would make new friends and have plenty of boyfriends, but it didn't help. I couldn't move beyond the feeling of missing them. Especially Rue. With time comes distance, space, and perspective. I began to realize that, with Trey, so much of our connection had been physical, chemical, and hormonal. But Rue had understood me. Every nuanced bit, down to my surprising foot odor that I never bothered to hide from her. And I had completely failed to pay attention to who she really was.

When I once again found myself home alone on a Friday night – dateless and friendless, but permanently this time – I decided to grab my purple lighter and head down to the basement. I wasn't going to summon another demon. I had learned my lesson and wasn't going to mess with those again. I would, however, seek the company of ghosts until the pain of my human heartbreak finally faded. Ghosts, after all, were a captive audience. Even if no one else was.

Bloody Mary

"It'll be okay. I promise! Don't be such a scaredy-cat!" Cerise reached out her tiny hand and prepared to drag me into the pitch-black guest bathroom. I didn't think I was susceptible to the peer pressure of a ten-year-old—someone less than half my age—but here we were. "Besides," she said, giving me that Cheshire grin of hers, "it's only a game."

I had been babysitting Cerise since she was born. Her mother and my stepmother attended all of the same high society galas around New York City, and my stepmother thought it would be good for me to learn a "hearty work ethic" from the age of thirteen. Not that my stepmother would know anything about that, having bounced from her senator father's Westchester mansion, to her financier first husband's spacious penthouse on Park Avenue, to my filmmaker father's converted warehouse in Tribeca. She worked as a wellness coach for a few wealthy housewives, but I had the feeling she didn't contribute much to our household bills. I also had the feeling that my appearance was such a dramatic contrast to hers, with my scrawny limbs, awkwardly angular features, bad skin, and frizzy hair, that she mostly wanted me out of her sight. She was conventionally pretty with a petite but perfect frame, an oil slick of black hair, olive skin, and a pink-bow of a mouth.

When Cerise was born, she immediately

acquired two things: an eccentric Francophile of a mother (just like my stepmother) and a dusting of fine red hair. And so the name Cerise—French for cherry—came to be. That red hair had continued to grow until it evolved into bouncy curls that shot out of her head like springs from a broken mattress, and her porcelain face had a light smattering of freckles. But my favorite of her features was her gopher-like front teeth. They protruded from her mouth and had a Wife of Bath–style gap between them. That girl could eat corn on the cob through a picket fence. I knew I had better enjoy them now, for soon enough her mom would be fitting her for braces to get those unruly teeth into perfect alignment.

I had grown quite attached to the little cherry blossom—Blossom, in fact, was my nickname for her—and she, to me. She had sobbed when I left for college on the opposite coast four years earlier. Truth be told, I had been a little heartbroken myself. So, when her mother, Andrea, called my dorm room and asked if I would look after Cerise for a month over the summer, I jumped at the chance. I wasn't due to start nursing school—a profession my father liked to remind me would prove less than lucrative—until September, and I figured I could leverage this experience into some padding for my resume. Besides, staying in their luxurious apartment on the Upper East Side was always a fringe benefit of spending time with Cerise. As for her parents, they would be sailing on a yacht in Greece with their billionaire friends, and as their usual nanny had to return to the Philippines to care for a sick relative, they thought it was best to leave

Cerise at home with me—especially as she is prone to seasickness.

So that was how I had found myself being tugged into a dark bathroom to play a ghost game. Cerise wanted to play a scary game with me, and while I was a big scaredy-cat when it came to anything even approaching the paranormal, I knew that my soft spot for Cerise would be larger than my fear and I would end up playing it with her. Bloody Mary. I hadn't played that game since a particularly, traumatic slumber party at the age of nine when my friend's brother barged into the bathroom wearing a wig, vampire fangs, and a coating of ketchup to scare us. He succeeded, and I had called my parents to come and get me. Mostly because I had wet my pants and didn't have another set of pajamas. At least this time there was no one else in the house that could scare us like that, and I was fairly confident about my bladder control.

I took her hand. "Okay. Let's do this."

Cerise had taken the taper candles from the dining room table and placed them on either side of the bathroom mirror. She, of course, was not allowed to play with matches, so I lit them for her. She had briefed me on the game instructions in that authoritative little tone of hers, and while they were different from the ones I had learned as a child, I figured she had done her homework.

"Okay. Now it's time for us to join blood." This idea made me a bit queasy, but if I was going to be a nurse, I would have to be more comfortable with blood. Cerise peeled off a bandage on her knee and picked at a particularly juicy scab until it bled. I found a razor in the medicine cabinet and lightly sliced the tip of my finger. I rubbed my bloody finger against her knee, and she replaced the bandage.

"Now you have to cross your arms over your heart like a mummy." I did as I was told. "Look straight into the mirror while I say the special words. Then, when I look at you, we are going to repeat her name three times." I nodded. She cleared her throat and made her eyes wide like a cartoon character. I tried not to giggle.

"Bloody Mary, come to me. Sacred friends, we shall be. Bloody Mary, with anger rare, wipes the blood onto her hair. Bloody Mary, it's our time. Listen, listen, to my rhyme." Cerise looked up at me and back to the mirror. Our voices seemed to almost harmonize: "Bloody Mary. Bloody Mary. Bloody Mary." I held my breath, half-expecting some ghostly woman to climb through the mirror and rip my head off. But there was nothing. Just the flicker of candlelight and the sound of Cerise and me breathing. Also, the scent of Andrea's freesia bathroom mist.

My stomach growled. We had been standing like mummies for several minutes, and I was ready to pop some popcorn and watch a movie. I looked at Cerise. She wasn't moving. She hardly seemed to be blinking. Whatever she was looking at in the mirror had her completely transfixed.

"Well, Blossom, I know you are mesmerized by your own beauty, but I think Bloody Mary isn't showing her face tonight." I uncrossed my arms and turned from the mirror to look at her. "We've got some popcorn and hot cocoa waiting for us. Whaddya say we head out to the living room? I'll let you pick the movie." Usually, these offers evoked a happy squeal from her, but she continued staring straight ahead. "Hello? Earth to Blossom? Let's get out of this dark bathroom." I reached out my hand to touch her shoulder and her head whipped around, bringing those gigantic eyes to look at mine. The look was unlike anything I had seen on her face before. It was wild. Angry. Her lips tremored into a slight snarl. I removed my hand; momentarily afraid she would bite me.

"Whoa! Blossom! Easy!"

Her eyes turned back to normal. She shook her head a bit and looked up at me. "Sorry. I...guess this just didn't work. Yeah. Let's go watch a movie."

"Are you ok? You seem...weird."

"I'm fine." She forced a brief smile and then opened the door and bounded down the hallway. I blew out the candles.

For a brief second, I thought I saw something flash across the mirror. I flipped the lights on. Nothing. Just to be on the safe side, I would keep that door shut for the rest of the night.

Tuesday was Cerise's swimming lesson, and after dropping her off I had some time to read trashy magazines and text with my friends from college about how much we missed each other already, and how this whole "adulting" thing was wildly overrated. When I walked from Central Park to pick up Cerise, she was, as usual, standing by herself, away from the mass of giggling girls who were also waiting for their nannies. I felt a pang of sympathy. I was always the kid who stood by herself, hoping that either I would disappear into the earth or my parents would pick me up before everyone else around me had a chance to sufficiently observe my painful awkwardness.

I waved to Cerise from the curb, but she didn't notice me. She was looking down at a puddle on the ground, leftover from the early morning summer storm. As I approached her, she shrugged her shoulders and said, "I don't know."

"You don't know what, Blossom?" She turned her focus to me, almost shocked to see me there, even though I knew she was expecting me. "Oh, uh, hi! I was just thinking that I don't know what I want to eat for lunch."

"Ah. Well, problem solved. I got us a lunch reservation at Sushi Samba!" Cerise clapped and squealed. I could always win that kid over with food.

Later that night while I was continuing to pore over my magazines, Cerise was sitting with her legs tucked under her at her usual kitchen island stool perch, scribbling away on a drawing. She started whistling a tune that I didn't recognize. Normally I cannot abide whistling, but this tune was nice. Haunting, even.

"Where'd you learn that song?" Cerise jumped when I spoke. It was as if she had forgotten that I was in the room with her. I was beginning to take my own forgettable-ness personally.

"Oh...from a friend."

"Which friend?"

"Someone from swim class." She stopped drawing and looked up at me, only to see that I was giving her the side-eye. She didn't like any of the girls from swim class. Or any other class, for that matter. She giggled, hopped off the stool, and threw a decorative couch pillow at me. This, of course, prompted an epic pillow fight.

Later, after I put her to bed, I came back down to the kitchen to clean up. Her drawing was still sitting where she left it. She had colored the entire page with a black marker, leaving only a white shape in the middle. I couldn't quite make it out, but it looked like a woman wearing a dress with long, spindly arms. I put everything back in Cerise's art cabinet, poured myself a glass of whatever fancy French wine Andrea left lying around, grabbed the rest of the popcorn, and headed to the guest room where an episode of *Real Housewives* was waiting. It would also be a perfect night for a glycolic acid mask with natural lavender.

After situating everything on the nightstand, I went into the en suite bathroom to prepare my mask. Once it was fully slathered over every inch of my face, a tiny bit got in my eye and I did my best to dab it with a wet washcloth. But it still burned.

"Fuck!" I yelled to no one in particular as I tried to manage the tears welling up in my eyes and the snot escaping from my nose while trying not to mess up the mask too badly. When I was finally dry enough, and could at least somewhat see out my eye again, I flipped off the bathroom light. There, in the

103

mirror, was a woman. I gasped and flipped the light back on. Nothing was there. When I turned it off again, she was gone. I looked around the bathroom, trying to figure out what, other than my imagination, might have caused that reflection. But that was the strange thing. I didn't see her for very long, but it was as if she had been actually *in* the mirror, the way a character is on a TV screen, and not a reflection. And she was smiling—no, *smirking*. I dabbed at my eye again, as it must have been the culprit with its blurry mess of chemicals obscuring my vision. Plus, Cerise's creepy game had clearly gotten to me.

The next morning at breakfast, I noticed a long scratch across Cerise's left cheek. "What happened, Blossom?" I asked while touching it with my finger. She winced a little.

"Oh, I scratched myself in my sleep." I picked up her hand to look at her nails. They were growing out a little but otherwise seemed safe to be in the proximity of a sleeping face.

"Well, the only way that we can make sure this doesn't happen again is for us to get emergency manicures, right now!" Cerise rolled her eyes. She hated manicures. Really, she hated any activity that required her to sit still for an extended period of time.

When we got to the nail salon, I pulled out chairs right next to each other for both of us. Cerise looked at the chair and blanched a little—which was surprising, considering that she already had the palest complexion I had ever seen.

"What's up, Blossom? Have a seat."

"Um…" she began fidgeting with her curls and wrapping them around her fingers. She always did this when she was nervous. "I'm going to sit over here." She chose a chair across the room from me.

"What's the matter? Do I smell?"

Cerise gave me a half laugh and retreated to the other side of the room. I shrugged and started my gel manicure. The smell of the various chemicals always made me woozy. I tried not to breathe too deeply.

I started to go into my usual manicure mental haze. There was nothing to read or look at, and my hands were indisposed. And so, I was left alone with my thoughts. I was missing my college friends, remembering how we had all huddled together in the pouring rain after graduation, vowing to see each other every six months. I knew that eventually would turn into once a year, and then once every few years, and then only at reunions. A painful twinge rose in my chest with this thought. But we'd always have those years and that goodbye before everything had to change. My hair and my graduation gown were soaking wet….

My eyes, left to their own devices while my mind was busy, drifted to the mirror on the wall behind my nail technician. I was snapped out of my reverie. In the mirror—no, on the mirror—was the woman I had seen the night before, this time in the full light of day. I jolted, and the nail technician gave me a *tsk* through her surgical mask. The woman was dressed in white. Her mouth spread into that smirk, and as it did, a thick ribbon of dark liquid spilled from it and oozed onto her dress. Blood.

When I woke up, the panicked nail technician's face was mere inches away from mine. I had fainted. She slapped my cheeks a few times before leaving to retrieve water for me. Cerise was standing over me, looking visibly upset and twirling her hair around her fingers so quickly I thought she would pull her curls right off of her head.

"This is all my fault." Cerise wailed and buried her face in her hands.

"What?"

In another moment, I was surrounded by a flurry of nail technicians. One was propping my head up, another was pouring water down my throat, and a third was fanning me with a folded newspaper. Only when they were thoroughly convinced I could stand on my own without falling over could the manicure continue. The headache was like a penny plonking around in my skull, tearing gray matter as it traveled. My ears were ringing.

Whatever we had conjured that night, it was real. Either that or I was going completely insane. I needed to take a breath and collect more data without alarming Cerise. But first, I needed a nap.

When we got home, I told Cerise she could pick a parent-approved movie. She nodded, looking at me with her eyes wide as if she feared I would fall right over again. I gave her a soft punch on her shoulder. "Don't worry about me. It's just a headache. And, hey, this wasn't your fault at all. It was my idea to get the manicures." She stared at me again, her eyes wide with worry, and I expected a hug. Instead, she turned on her heel and took quick, shuffling steps to the TV. I poured myself a huge glass of water, retrieved one of Andrea's special painkillers from their secret spot in the cupboard, and headed off to bed.

When I woke up, the guest room was dark. Somehow, I had slept for three hours, even though I swore I had set my alarm to go off in one. Clearly, it was the painkillers. The guest bedroom was just off the kitchen, which was next to the family room. I could see that the television was on, but Cerise was nowhere to be seen. I walked up the stairs to the second floor of the apartment and could see that the light was on in Cerise's bedroom, and a slice of it slipped into the hallway from under her door.

A wary feeling bubbled up my brainstem, and I felt the urge to tiptoe, which made no real sense. When I got to her door, I could hear her singing. It was the same tune she had been whistling the day before, but this time it had words. However, I couldn't make any of them out. I wasn't even entirely sure they were English.

I knocked. "Blossom? Are you okay in there?"

"Yeah. I'm fine. DON'T COME IN!"

The urgency in her voice was alarming and my babysitting instincts were on alert. This was a kid who never told me to get out of her room. Who, in fact, often made me wait to leave until she was asleep after putting her to bed at night. I swung open the door and she looked at me guiltily. She was sitting on the floor in the middle of a circle of items. There was a lit candle (which made me angry because she was absolutely not allowed to use matches or lighters), some salt, a spool of twine, a large quartz crystal from Andrea's collection, some rosemary sprigs, and a huge knife (she was also not allowed to touch knives). I didn't have time to process this circle because her arms and legs were covered in small cuts and scratches that were bleeding. Something was terribly wrong. And there, in Cerise's full-length mirror, staring at me, was Bloody Mary.

Before my brain could react, my feet were running across the room. I scooped Cerise up and brought her across the hall to the bathroom where I started dabbing at her wounds with a towel. They were small and shallow cuts, thankfully, and they would heal quickly. As I cleared the blood away, I saw that they were in perfect little zigzags all up and down her arms and legs. My heart started racing.

"What are you doing? What are you doing? STOP!" She yelled, pushing herself away from me. Those stick arms were surprisingly strong.

"Blossom, you're bleeding…"

"You interrupted! Now she's going to be MAD!"

"Who?"

Cerise crumpled to the floor, curled up in a ball, and buried her face in her hands. "Bloody Mary," she said through her palms.

I kept dabbing the cuts I could get to in her position on the floor.

"Blossom, I'm so sorry I let you play that game. I never should have. Listen," I said, gently guiding her to a seated position on the floor. She uncovered her face and looked at me. I continued softly, "Cerise, Bloody Mary isn't real. It's just a game. There's no such thing as a ghost in a mirror that can hurt you." I didn't believe my own words, but I knew I had to say them.

She narrowed her eyes at me. "You've seen her too. I know you have. She told me. That's why you fainted when you were getting your nails done."

I stroked her head in an attempt to get her to calm down. Her hair was crazed and popping, just like her eyes. She raised them up and looked at the mirror over the sink. An expression of recognition hovered on her porcelain face for just a moment. She was looking at someone. I whirled my head around. Bloody Mary was in the mirror, staring at us, that dark liquid spilling from her mouth and spreading over her white dress. Her hair was gray and fell in thin strands around her face. And that smirk. She started moving her arms erratically like her elbows were being pulled by puppet strings. Her head began to shake back and forth, and I didn't want to wait and see what she was going to do next. I screamed before I could stop myself, scooped Cerise up in my arms, and ran out of the room.

"Shh, shh. It's going to be okay—" I wasn't sure if I was talking to her or to myself.

We burst through the one room in the apartment that was always off-limits: The Master Bedroom. It smelled musty from having not been exposed to any air for almost three weeks.

We ducked into Andrea's walk-in closet, turned on the light, and shut the door behind us. The glare from the many pairs of jeweled Louboutins with their lacquered red soles was almost blinding.

"Bloody Mary can't find us in here because there is nothing that makes a reflection," I told her. I glanced around at the gold fixtures, and a veritable wall of gold accessories, but I was still confident that we would be safe there.

Cerise was shaking. "Bloody Mary is real. She's REAL. And I called her that night. At first, she was nice to me. But then she came into my room at night and didn't let me sleep. And now, she's...making me do things."

"What things, Blossom?"

"Well," she covered her face with her hands again for a moment, "she taught me that song. And she can scratch me with her mind. And if I do the things she tells me to do, she can come out of the mirror and be free. And if not..." She burst into tears.

"Blossom, I need you to tell me. I believe you." A panicked feeling choked my throat, making it hard to speak. I had to steady my voice. I couldn't let her know my fear. I started stroking her head again, forcing my hand to stay soft and calm. "What happens if you don't free her?"

"She's going to kill you!" she wailed. Cerise crawled into my lap and I rocked her.

Being victimized by other women was not an unfamiliar feeling. I was, after all, the ugly theater kid at Brearley—a prestigious, all-girls school on the Upper East Side of Manhattan. It didn't matter whether I replaced my glasses with contacts, how many Cartier Love Bracelets I stacked on my wrist, how many clubs I joined, or how many drugs I tried. I was still the gawky teacher's pet who was six inches taller than everyone else and was, at the very least, a punchline. And, at the very most, a victim of brutal hazing. I spent weekends locked away in my room, wishing for the tribe of friends that would finally arrive in college. In the era of "women supporting women" that every Instagram page seemed to espouse, I could say that my high school years failed dismally in that regard. In fact, most of my close high school friends had attended St. Bernard's—an equally prestigious all-boys school. I met them through debate and theater competitions, and they were far more kind and respectful than any of the classmates at my school were.

My hair stood on end. I realized why I had passed out. Yes, I had been scared. Of course. But there was something else as well. That smirk. It had been all too familiar. That evil smile when one's pleasure is derived entirely from someone else's pain. The expression of the smug bully. It was a look I had seen splashed across too many faces, too many times. I rested my head on Cerise's, who had stopped crying and now seemed frozen. Powerless.

"Ouch!" Cerise screamed and I pulled away from her, worried that I had accidentally hurt her. There on her forearm was a freshly scratched letter M, and it was bleeding.

"Oh my God, Cerise! Did she just do this to you?"

"Yes, I told you. She can scratch me with her mind! And she's not going to stop! She wants me to free her from the mirror!"

Ok. Enough was enough. I was officially pissed. I was done being bullied. I would never let anyone else make me feel powerless again. Not only that, I absolutely would not allow Cerise to be bullied either. I held her head between my palms. She was breathing rapidly like a scared little rabbit.

"Listen. I'm not going to let her keep hurting you. We are going to stop her. And you know what? Just because someone tells you to do something, that doesn't mean you have to do it. No one else is the boss of you. And if someone tells you that you have to be or look a certain way, or do things that you don't want to do, well…FUCK THEM."

Cerise recoiled. "You have to put a dollar in the swear jar."

"Fine. Best money I've spent all year. I'll put another two in. FUCK THEM. FUCK THEM!"

Cerise covered her face again, this time so that I wouldn't see her blushing.

"I'm sorry we played the game, Blossom. But you didn't do anything wrong, and I know if we work together, we will find a way to stop her."

She looked at me with those watery green eyes. "Do you promise?"

"Absolutely."

We ran downstairs to the guest bedroom, and I grabbed my phone. While it was still a reflective surface, I figured it was less so than a computer screen. How to get rid of Bloody Mary. The Google search mainly offered options about how the Bloody Mary cocktail can get rid of hangovers, but I eventually found advice for getting rid of the entity.

Just as I had finished scrolling through the instructions, I heard a groaning sound resonating throughout the apartment, as if the walls had been transformed into wounded beasts. The noise culminated in a high-pitched squeal, like steam fighting through a radiator, and we both covered our ears. After a few excruciating moments, everything was silent.

"Um...you know how...water makes reflections?" Cerise asked as she slowly uncovered her ears.

"Yeah..." I said, dreading where her thoughts were leading us.

"She's...she's in the pipes."

"Yes. Yes, she is."

I gave the instructions to Cerise, and we quickly got to work. As we did, I could hear the spirit moving through the walls like some kind of colossal rodent, scraping and oozing her way around the apartment. The stench of death rose up from all of the drains, and I received momentary pleasure from visualizing Mary crawling through years of rodent and cockroach carcasses, plus the occasional ball of hair clogging the pipes.

We grabbed towels and blankets and covered all of the mirrors in the house as quickly as we could, turning on the lights as we went. That step felt futile, as Mary had made herself seen in well-lit rooms, but the reassurance the light provided was helpful, nonetheless. As we worked, Cerise acquired new scratches all over her body. Luckily, they weren't very deep, but they inspired a sense of urgency and I worked even more quickly. I needed to make them stop.

Cerise went into the Master Bathroom, climbed up on the sink, and taped towels over the vanity mirrors, and I stayed in the bedroom covering the floor-to-ceiling closet mirrors. The only sound either of us could hear was the pulling and ripping of duct tape. But then, I heard a splash and Cerise was screaming. Only it wasn't a normal scream. The sound was garbled. As if it was traveling through water.

A stream of water was gushing from the faucet. It had traveled from the sink to the floor, and it had widened and morphed into a human form. Bloody Mary was suspended in a bell jar shape of moving water. She was holding Cerise by the throat and pinning her against the wall. I did the only thing I could think of: I turned off the faucet. In an instant, Bloody Mary was reduced to droplets, and both she and Cerise ended up in a puddle on the floor. I picked up Cerise, shut the door behind me, and we scrambled back into the safety of the walk-in closet.

"Blossom, are you ok? Are you hurt?" Cerise both nodded and shook her head. She was shaking. I could see that she had a fresh cut on her cheek. "Listen. I want you to stay here, okay? I will finish covering up the mirrors and getting rid of Bloody Mary. I just need you to stay put. Promise me."

Cerise nodded reluctantly. I handed her my phone.

"If anything happens, if I don't come back for you in a half-hour, I want you to call the police. Promise me you will."

"I will. I promise."

We stared at each other for a moment and then hugged. When I stood up, I had a renewed sense of urgency and resolve. I frantically resumed the work of covering the mirrors, not giving Bloody Mary's image time to materialize in any of them. I then dropped the electronic shades over the windows, and, for good measure, covered up the TV in the family room. When all of the mirrors were covered—or, rather, all but *one*—I was ready.

I went into the guest bathroom just off the kitchen, the one where we had originally played the game, and where I had left the mirror uncovered. I closed the door, lit a candle, and turned off the light. After crossing my arms over my chest, I took a deep breath and said Bloody Mary's name three times.

She didn't appear. *Coward.*

"Bloody Mary, you need to leave! You are not welcome here! Go back where you came from! No one wants you here!!"

The ground and walls began to rumble. All at once, every single faucet in the apartment spewed a deluge of water. I pushed open the bathroom door and there she was in the kitchen, in that same bell jar of water as she had been when she pinned Cerise to the wall.

"Holy shi—" I started to say, as she lunged at me. I dove out of her way. She splashed against the cupboards and disappeared. But only for a moment. I had to keep her away from Cerise, no matter what.

"Oh, is that all you got? You're water! And a reflection! You're nothing! You don't scare me!" I didn't mean that. I was extremely scared of her. But I had seen enough movies to know that the villains can't help being baited by taunts.

Slowly, she rose again from the water that was still rushing from the faucet. I reached for the faucet to turn it off but she was too fast and pushed me against the island. She wasn't going to let that happen again. The water was starting to cover the floor. The floor! Maybe if I made it to the shag rug in the living room, she wouldn't be able to follow me because she wouldn't be able to move across an absorbent surface. It was a stretch, but I had to try it.

I had only taken a few steps when I felt water rushing around my ankle, pulling my foot out from under me. I landed on my stomach with a hard thud and let out an involuntary shriek. Bloody Mary's hand squeezed my ankle so tightly I could feel my tendons pop as she dragged me back into the kitchen. The floor was slick with water and there was nothing I could leverage against to escape her grip. She flipped me onto my back and then moved onto my legs, trapping them. Somehow, she moved so slowly, even as the water that sustained her rushed so quickly. Her head came closer and closer to mine, and my entire body was soon covered in water. I had no idea that water could be so repressively heavy.

Her mouth was inches away from mine, and she released from it the hot oozing liquid that I had seen in the mirror. It covered my mouth and nose, and sloshed around in my throat, making it impossible to breathe. I gasped and struggled, but it was useless. I thrashed and fought like a dying fish, but the liquid just seemed to thicken, blocking my airways entirely. My survival instincts surged one more time, forcing my limbs into movement. But then, upon realizing that my body was overpowered, everything within it started to give up. My ears filled with rushing water and gargling sounds. And even those sounds started to become more and more muffled as my senses weakened, my pulse started to slow, and my brain started to shut down.

As quickly as the water had started, it stopped. All the faucets stopped running. Bloody Mary was gone, and so was the deadly liquid. I gasped and spat and coughed. My breath seemed to want to take its sweet time refilling my lungs, almost as if it didn't trust them. As the adrenaline wore off I became queasy and shaky. I barfed Mary's dark ooze all over the wet kitchen floor. I needed to end this. And I knew that there was only one place in the apartment where she could go.

I peeled myself off the floor and limped back into the guest bathroom. Bloody Mary was already there in the mirror, waiting for me, and wearing her blood-stained white dress. And her smirk.

That fucking smirk.

Before I could stop myself, I pulled my arm back and delivered a jab to the mirror, causing it to crack and sending a painful sensation screaming up my arm. My knuckles started to bleed. This was not going to be an effective strategy. I grabbed the decorative marble elephant from its place on the sink and continued hitting the mirror until it shattered into a violent mosaic, and a few big shards were torpedoed to the ground. She remained in the mirror, refracted into a zillion pieces. Powerless.

I had never stood up to any of my bullies. I never quite knew how to, and those wounds sat inside of me like fragile porcelain dolls. I kept them on an interior shelf deep within my psyche, afraid of disturbing them in case they were to shatter and cut my insides. And so those wounded dolls stayed there, observing me through gleaming glass eyes, somehow wickedly sentient, not allowing me to move freely through my own memories. I decided that Bloody Mary would not be adding anything to that collection.

"You are not welcome here! No one wants you! GET OUT!" Just then I couldn't quite remember what the actual words were that you were supposed to say to get rid of Blood Mary, but these felt right to me.

Maybe it was because she was literally in pieces, or maybe it was because I felt inhumanly strong after shattering the mirror, or maybe my entire nervous system was just utterly shot after almost drowning. But I wasn't scared of her anymore.

"Go bother someone else." I rubbed my sore knuckles. "Or, better yet, follow the pipes to the river, and follow the river to the ocean. Spend eternity with the fucking dolphins and stop picking on little kids. Heal whatever wound trapped you in that mirror in the first place." I turned on the lights, and she was gone. When I turned them off again, only the splintered reflection of the candle remained before I blew it out.

And, with that, I left the bathroom, slamming the door a little for effect.

Cerise was standing at the apartment door speaking to a stricken super, who was surveying the flooded mess. She ran to me and jumped into my arms.

"Is she gone?"

"Yes. And she's not going to bother you anymore."

Cerise released her grip and shimmied off of me. "When the water started rushing and wouldn't stop, I called the super and told him to shut off the water to our apartment right away," she said, looking bashful in an attempt to hide how proud of herself she really was. "I guess even a ghost is no match for the super." She shrugged, and her Cheshire grin made its appearance. I high-fived her with my good hand.

"You are one smart kid."

The cleanup took several days, and I paid for the mirror replacement with the ample "emergency fund" cash that Andrea always left for me. My ankle was bruised and tender, but it was nothing a little ice and a bandage couldn't fix. By the time Cerise's parents returned home, all trace of damage was gone. Cerise's cuts had healed, and I had to leave the relative safety of the luxurious apartment where I had battled a ghost to do something truly terrifying: start my first real job and my new life as a real adult. But I promised I would still babysit.

My promise to Cerise that Bloody Mary wouldn't bother her anymore held true. But, for me, she still pops up every once in a while. She doesn't say or do anything. Her smirking face just hovers for a few minutes, checking up on me in my bathroom mirror in much the same way I'd wager the girls I went to high school check up on me through social media. And, like those girls, she occupies my mental space only briefly, and I carry on with my life.

The Telephone Game

It is hard to imagine the world before the iPhone. And it is hard to imagine my life before playing the telephone game.

When I went to grad school it was a world of flip phones and T9 texting—outdated technology that seems so innocuous now. And yet, at the time, it proved to be anything but.

The setting of my grad school years was none other than Harvard University, where I would acquire a graduate degree in linguistics. It was also where I would acquire a group of friends to whom I became intensely connected right off the bat during our wide-eyed orientation week.

We had all found ourselves standing guard at the open bar during the new student get-together under a fancy tent. We seemed to all have a penchant for prosecco and brie cheese, and the conversation quickly migrated to various nerdy topics: language theorists, Derrida, and board games. While our circle had started out with at least a dozen people, eventually the superfluous folks grew tired of our conversation and we were left with just the seven of us. And so, it would remain.

There was me, of course, but everyone referred to me as "Bomb"—the word that T9 presented as the primary option when texting my name, which was Anna. And then there was Thea, the athlete of the group and captain of the kickball team whose seriousness was contagious. Thankfully, her presence made us all fall in line, instead of squandering our education on games of flip cup. There was Robin, who we called Danza because she was convinced that the lyrics to "Hold Me Closer Tiny Dancer" were actually "Hold Me Closer Tony Danza." There was Mira, with her mane of dark blonde hair who could—and often would—drink us all under the table. There was Bethany, who was both a former theater major and sorority sister, and who still wore the mantle of both. And then, there was a set of twins—Eden and Elle—they were like something out of a sitcom with their good looks, enthusiasm, and penchant for boy drama.

Over the course of the next two years, we would learn about language, the brain, context, and culture. We would learn that there is, in fact, such a thing as a stupid question. And a deadly one.

Fall in Massachusetts was particularly lovely. Crisp, colorful, and providing an excuse to don my wardrobe fixtures of V-neck cardigans and tall riding boots. It also, of course, provided an excuse for consuming everything pumpkin. Classes moved beyond their introductory sessions and into a frenetic pace, which was reflected in the urgency with which students traveled from one place to another. My friends and I had spent September and October hunched over books in a library, and so when Halloween rolled around, in spite of my nerdy proclivities, I was ready to party. Preferably while wearing a toga.

Cronkhite, the graduate student dorm where Bethany lived, was hosting a party that night, and the group of us strolled into the dining hall-turned-party space like bedsheet adorned royalty. We would hold court, dominate the room, and be crowned the Flip Cup Champions. We would dance in a tight circle to Bethany's playlist that blared from the speakers, forming our own island in the middle of the ebbing and flowing movement of drunken bodies. Everyone needed to blow off some steam that night it seemed.

After my fourteenth beer, a few hours of staggering, and explaining the term "beer goggles" to an international student (as I was wearing actual plastic beer goggles), Bethany pulled us all into the bathroom, made sure no one else was in there and told us to huddle up.

"You guysssss. You guys. There's this thing. There's this thing we gotta do. This game we gotta play. We totally gotta do it." My perception was a bit fuzzy, but there was definitely some woo-ing and high five-ing. "Let's do it!" Danza yelled.

Bethany instructed us to grab our flip phones and follow her to Harvard Yard in the large open space in front of John Harvard's statue—the one whose left foot hundreds of tourists rub each year for luck, and just as many students drunkenly desecrate with bodily fluids.

The Yard was peppered with the sounds of dorm parties, and a few students were making out in dark doorways, but we mostly had it all to ourselves. My buzz was starting to shift into fatigue and headache, but I was intrigued by what Bethany had in mind for us. The seven of us—Bethany, Thea, Mira, Danza, Eden, Elle, and me—were joined by three other drunk grad students that

Bethany had recruited, because apparently, the game required ten people.

We formed a circle – our bedsheet togas were inadequate against the chill of the grass as we sat down – and Bethany's voice dipped into a hushed, serious tone as she began her instructions. She had been a teacher before coming to grad school, and I had no trouble believing that she could command a room of unwieldy middle schoolers.

"We are about to play the telephone game, which will allow us to conjure a spirit known as The Answer Man. Some people say that it's dangerous, but my roommate in college played it and nothing bad happened. Not only that, but she got some answers to her important questions. So, everyone needs to do two things right now," she sat up straight and gave us her teacher face to make sure we were all listening.

"First, think of a question—a burning one. One that you *need* to know the answer to. One that matters *deeply to your life and entire existence*." Sheesh. No pressure. My question was definitely burning, though in no way was it crucial to my entire existence.

"Next, look at the person to your left and make sure you have that person's number in your phone." Danza was to my left. We high-fived and she snickered. I was fairly certain she was buying exactly none of this and was just following the whims of the group after too much beer. "Give me a thumbs up when you are ready to continue." I had to suppress an eye roll at Bethany's teacherly ways but gave my thumbs up nonetheless.

"Ok. On my signal, you will call the person to your left. Everyone's phone should go straight to voicemail since the line will obviously be busy. Everyone's except for one." Bethany's eyes grew wide. I found myself feeling suddenly nervous and wondering if this was the best idea, given everyone's state of intoxication. "One person's call will be picked up by The Answer Man." Bethany scanned the group, gauging our reactions. Danza began shifting nervously next to me. Bethany lifted a scolding finger and continued. "We have to do the ritual exactly as I have described or else it won't work. There are three important rules: first, if you speak with The Answer Man, do not take him up on his offer to stay on the line in exchange for more information. Ask your question, get your answer, thank him, and wait. He will ask you a question in return for answering yours which brings us to the second rule: you MUST answer his question, no matter what. Third, and most importantly, do not hang up on The Answer Man. He hates that."

Elle tentatively raised her hand, and Bethany pointed at her. "What happens if we don't follow the rules?"

"That is not even an option. We must follow all of the rules, no matter what." Once again, Bethany scanned the group, and upon seeing some nervous and reluctant faces, she laughed and took a relaxed posture. She needed to put everyone at ease so that no one would leave, as losing participants would mean that the game would not work. "Listen, guys, I promise everything will be fine. Let's just give it a try, and all agree to follow the rules, ok? No big deal." There seemed to be something tugging at her voice. A kind of desperation.

Mira, ever the adventurous one (who also happened to be significantly drunker than the rest of us) blurted out her encouragement. "Don't be pansies! Let's play this fuckin' game and get our fuckin' questions answered!" She took a hearty swallow from the beer bottle she had snuck out of the party, draining it. "My question is where to find more beer...."

"You're sure we'll be ok...." Eden looked at Bethany sternly and tried to wiggle out from under Mira's arm that had found itself slung over her shoulder. I finally decided it was time to chime in.

"Are there any guarantees in life, if we think about it?" I said, pushing myself up from the ground and onto my feet. I pulled myself into my best Norma Ray stance. "We could all die tomorrow, and then where would that leave us? Dead. Without having gotten our questions answered. So let's just do this. I, for one, have a burning question."

Bethany looked at me gratefully. Mira whooped and raised her empty beer bottle. And with that, the matter was settled.

We reformed our tight circle, sitting with our knees touching. On Bethany's cue, we would call the person to our left. Whatever happened after that was up to The Answer Man. Ten flip phones creaked open, and ten thumbs hovered over the green call button, waiting. Harvard Yard was quiet and dark. It would have felt peaceful if there wasn't something else. An eerie, foreboding feeling. I shivered.

"Ok. On my signal." Bethany raised her arm above her head as if she was about to start a drag race. "Three, two, one, NOW!" We all pressed call, brought our phones to our ears in almost perfect unison, and waited. I felt a pang of disappointment when I heard Danza's voice on her voicemail greeting.

Directly across the circle from me, looking almost angelic in her backlit toga, Bethany rose to her feet, eyes wide, clutching her phone with both hands.

"Oh my god, is it really you? I knew you'd answer!"

"Shut the fuck up, Bethany. Obviously, you are faking." I couldn't tell what was more surprising in that moment: the fact that Bethany was possibly on the phone with an omniscient entity, or that Eden had cursed. Bethany's eyes darted and flashed. I hadn't known her long, but I considered myself to be an excellent judge of nonverbal body language. Based on how she was holding herself and the expression on her face, I could tell she wasn't faking.

"I have my question for you: is my mom going to be ok? Are her cancer treatments going to work? We've heard so many different things from different doctors, and...."

We looked around the circle at one another, bewildered. She hadn't shared that information with any of us. And was she really talking to The Answer Man? I could tell that some people weren't buying it. But I knew Bethany. She was far too earnest and practical to pull a prank on this level. As I watched, she covered her eyes with her hand, nodding and listening.

"Oh, come ON –" Eden started to protest and I shushed her. I felt my adrenaline start to surge. This was real. A ball in my stomach began to unfurl, sending excited yet nervous fingers through my bloodstream.

"Oh, thank god. Thank you. I've been so scared." Bethany continued speaking, her voice refracted through the well of tears gathering in her throat. "Yes, I'm ready for my question." She uncovered her eyes, and they were suddenly wide. She slowly looked around the circle at each one of us before simply saying one word: "No." And then, "Yes. She's here."

For a few agonizing seconds, Bethany's eyes lingered on each of us, and I could tell that my same nervous feelings were creeping under everyone else's skin. Finally, she looked at me.

"Her name's Anna." It was the first time in months that a friend had called me by my real name. Somehow my brain could only focus on how jarring that sounded and not on the fact that The Answer Man had asked to speak with me. I felt Danza grip my wrist. Bethany held out the phone. "Anna, he wants to talk to you."

Adrenaline is activated during moments of extreme fear, and it causes tunnel vision—a survival mechanism built into our fight or flight system that allows our eyes to seek out and focus on escape routes. My vision was narrowed so that all I could see was Bethany. There was no Harvard Yard and no other people in the circle. Just Bethany, me, and whatever was on the other end of the phone. Had my vision not been so hyper-focused I would have seen my friends' terrified faces or watched the three random students run back to the safety of the dorm kegger. But all I could see was the green glow of the phone, and all I could hear was my own breath coming fast and shallow. Somehow, I crossed the circle, took the phone from Bethany's hand, and put it to my ear.

There was a crackle and hiss, followed by a chattering sound, like teeth clicking together in the cold. And then, a voice.

"What is your question?" It was breathy, straining to speak, and there was something strangely soft to it. Not quite menacing, like I was expecting. I looked at Bethany, half hoping that she would collapse into laughter and tell me that the whole thing had been a prank, but she was locked in a sobbing hug with Thea. Something roiled in my gut.

My question dropped out of me before I could stop it. "Are Joseph and I going to end up together?" I kept my eyes looking at the ground. I knew I'd be met with shocked and disapproving glances, and I couldn't take it in that moment. I met Joseph earlier that summer when I first moved into my apartment. My lease started on July 1st, and even though I wasn't due to be on campus until late August, I wanted to get a jump start on moving in to get oriented to my new city. I was starving after a day of unpacking, and I wandered to The Plough and Stars—a delightful little hole in the wall—for a pub dinner. Joseph had been there playing trivia with his fellow nerds, and he sidled up beside me and bought me a drink.

No one liked Joseph. He didn't treat me particularly well, but I tolerated it because I was utterly smitten. I couldn't help it. He would bail on dates without calling, and there was one time when he invited me on a "group outing" that was ostensibly a "blind date" for him and another girl, and I had apparently been invited along for moral support. I didn't speak to him for two weeks after that, but it didn't seem to faze him. He was charming in a corn-fed midwestern way and was already a professor at Harvard Business School by the age of thirty. He had smarts, a myriad of passions and hobbies, spoke four different languages, and had one thing I didn't: a stable home life. He just didn't have a lot of hair. But I knew he was my soulmate. I just *knew* it. The other silly stuff didn't seem to matter.

The Answer Man spoke again, wheezing his response. "He will place a large diamond on your finger. And he will betray you shortly after. What you do next is up to you. That is as much as I can tell you." I shook my head. I know a thing or two about trudging through betrayal. I wanted to know more about this diamond....

I could hear The Answer Man's teeth chattering, and I felt more giddy than scared. After all, I was going to end up with Joseph....

"What are the sins of your father?" he wheezed.

Shit. I knew he would ask about this. But my own question, and the beer, had clouded my judgment.

"What are the sins of your father?" he asked again. I looked around the circle, the same way Bethany had when he had asked her a question. Everyone was staring. I could not utter the words The Answer Man wanted. My family and I had already been shunned by our community at home. Reporters had kept my name out of the papers because I was a minor at the time, and all connections between my father and me had been scrubbed from the media. No one at Harvard knew anything about my father and the seeping, disgusting shame he had spattered over so many people. I could not speak the truth out loud. I would not. My peace had come at too high a price, and it had taken too long for me to find my tribe.

"No." My response seemed to echo through the Yard. Bethany dislodged her head from Thea's shoulder and looked at me quizzically. The voice on the other end of the phone started to ask the same question again, but instead of listening, I clicked the red button to end the call. I knew I would regret doing that. Bethany had been clear: answer The Answer Man's question and do not hang up on him. I had ignored both of those rules. But it was simply the best I could do at the moment. Everyone just looked at me, not sure what was going to happen next. I dropped the phone to the ground, suddenly not wanting it to be in my hand any longer. When Bethany spoke, her voice was hoarse. She rubbed her throat.

"Did you answer his question?" I nodded yes, lying. When I did the fingertips on both hands went numb and started to tingle, as if they were asleep. I needed to get home, drink a huge glass of water, and get a good night's sleep.

"Guys, I've gotta get out of here. I'm suddenly not feeling well." I didn't wait for anyone to respond and waved away all offers to walk me home over my shoulder as I strode out of the Yard. I lived one street over, with a nice little shortcut through the faculty club, so managing a safe walk home at that time of night would not be a problem. I poked my fingertips with my key before inserting it into the lock. They were still numb and tingling.

My grad student housing was a tiny studio apartment, and it had that kind of musty smell that old buildings do that I always found comforting. Having grown up in an old house, I associated that smell with the sanguine years of my childhood, before the bottom dropped out of my life and family.

Joseph's apartment was across a parking lot from mine, and I could see into it from my kitchen when his lights were on. When I checked, they were off. It was almost 3 a.m., which meant he must be asleep. This thought satisfied me, regardless of the fact that his bedroom shades were open. He always closed them before going to sleep.

Water and sleep. That is what you need. Water and sleep. After pounding two huge glasses of water, the tingling in my fingers stopped. I managed to swap my toga for fuzzy pajamas before flopping onto my bed—the entirety of which was coated in a shade of cotton candy pink. Grad school was something I had done for myself, and similarly, my bed was dressed according to my preferences and

132

mine alone. Sleep came quickly.

Harvard Square is always a crush of people, each moving with a different purpose and for a variety of reasons. Students rushing, tourists gawking, homeless youth begging, musicians playing. The knot of people by the Harvard Square T station and near the Daily News was Gordian in its scope and confusion, and I always used my messenger bag as a shield as I moved through it on my way to class. That day, though, everyone seemed to be moving more quickly than usual and no one blocked my path. I would make it to class early and maybe have time to text flirt with Joseph.

I almost collided with a child. He was dressed in a shade of powder blue, in an outfit that looked almost like a bad prom suit, and an upside-down salad bowl of dark hair topped a bone-white face. He raised his eyes to me – shades of gray and red, as pale blue irises floated in a pool of burst blood vessels – and his teeth began chattering. My initial instinct was to wrap my arms around his frail frame to warm him. Before I could, he pointed at me. His mouth opened. He wheezed and coughed. And then, "WHAT ARE THE SINS OF YOUR FATHER?"

He grabbed my left hand, brought it to his mouth, and I passed out.

When I woke up, I was still in my bed. But instead of pink, the sheets and comforter were a deep, meaty shade of purple. Blood. My blood.

"Fuck!"

I was so focused on sopping up the mess that it took several minutes for the pain to set in and the source of the bleeding to reveal itself. The nail on my right pinky had peeled completely off and a deep cut bisected the tip of my finger. The blood just kept coming.

"Shit!"

Could someone bleed out from a finger injury? I swaddled my pinky in half a roll of toilet paper and covered it in a hand towel while rocking back and forth on the black and white tile of the bathroom floor, begging it to stop. When I pulled back my amateur mummification, I could see that the cut had split to reveal a frosty tip of bone. I needed medical attention.

Saturday after Halloween in the emergency room was like a zombie apocalypse of drunken mistakes. The only explanation I could provide for the doctor was that I had done something in my intoxicated state of sleep. I had a history of doing strange things in my sleep, in fact, and had been known to sleepwalk on occasion. But I knew there had to be a connection between the kid in my dream and my injury. After all, he had asked The Answer Man's question and grabbed my hand just before I woke up in a pool of my own blood….

"And you don't remember anything? You didn't wake up at all?" the puzzled intern asked while examining my hand. I shook my head. Somehow telling her about a nightmare that had learned to leap the boundary between dreamland and reality didn't feel like the right thing to do. I just wanted to get out of there and not have to stay for a full psych workup on top of everything else.

I received stitches and could expect scarring. My nail would take at least six months to grow back. The intern recommended aloe vera and shea butter for keeping my skin moisturized and helping it to heal. She bandaged my finger and gave me a mild painkiller, and I lugged my massive pinky home. Maybe I had just experienced a weird sleepwalking episode after all, and the nightmare was purely coincidental. That's what I told myself as I put clean sheets on the bed and got ready to hop back in it. After popping a pill I fell asleep on and off until Monday morning.

The sleep was dreamless. Thank goodness.

When I got to class on Monday morning, Thea was already wearing her signature intense facial expression – set eyes and no trace of a smile. I took the seat next to her and she leaned in toward me, her tone of voice matching her face.

"I'm worried about Bethany. Jesus! What happened to your hand?"

"I cut it on something while I was asleep."

"Do you sleep with your kitchen knives?" She grabbed my hand to further examine my bandage.

"No. I, um, do weird things when I sleep." *Like getting my finger gnawed off by a super terrifying kid.* "It's fine. Why are you worried about Bethany?" I pulled my hand back, eager to change the subject.

"Well, she was complaining about a sore throat. I mean, not sore exactly. She said it felt numb. And it was tingling. Almost like it was asleep."

A chill blasted my nervous system and I shifted in my seat. "What do you mean?" I said with a little too much urgency in my voice. Those symptoms were sounding familiar....

"I don't know. I even consulted Dr. Google, and a numb throat, well, isn't really a thing unless you have a spinal cord injury."

"Are you sure she doesn't?" I asked, unhelpfully.

"I'm not sure of anything. I tried to convince her to visit the student health center, but she said that she wasn't sick and her spine wasn't injured. Her throat was just numb and she couldn't explain it. It was even impacting her voice and she could barely speak."

"It sounds like she might just be coming down with something, like laryngitis maybe?" I was trying to convince myself that there was a normal and perfectly logical medical explanation for Bethany's symptoms.

We paused our conversation as our professor made her entrance, as it was always an event. She was known for boisterous leggings and miniskirts, topped with a cottony pouf of white hair. Today her leggings were orange and brown plaid, peppered with tiny pumpkins. Fall themed, naturally.

Thea turned back to me. "Because the last time I talked to her, she said, 'I didn't tell the truth. I'm sorry, and I love you.' What the hell does that mean?"

I shrugged and looked straight ahead as our professor began her lecture. I was getting an uncomfortable feeling in my stomach—not unlike the tingling that I experienced in my fingers—that I did my best to ignore.

Thea leaned in closer to me and brought her

voice to a whisper. "But here's the other thing. She hasn't returned any of my calls or texts since yesterday afternoon. And as you can clearly see, she's not in class today. That is not like her at all."

"Well, that proves it! She's sick. It's nothing to worry about," I said with a forced sparkle in my voice.

Thea gave me a quick side-eye before opening her notebook to a blank page. "Come on. We always text each other when we're missing class. Always. Remember that one time when she had food poisoning from the dorm cafeteria? She still managed to text. She always texts."

Thea had me there. Maybe she was right. Class seemed to drone on forever. When it finally ended I grabbed Thea by the arm with my good hand. "Listen, you might be right. I think we should go check on her." Thea nodded in agreement, and for a brief moment, her eyes seemed to be searching mine. Something flashed across hers and then she looked down at my injured pinkie. I knew that there was no possible way that she was making a connection that I didn't want her to make, but I couldn't be completely sure. The Answer Man had spoken to both Bethany and me. I had an injury on my finger, and Bethany appeared to have a numb throat.

I started to feel undeniable panic as we wordlessly accelerated our pace en route to Cronkhite. My finger throbbed as we walked, and questions pounded inside of my head. Bethany told Thea that she hadn't answered the question. I wouldn't admit it to Thea just then, and I pushed the thought away, but I hadn't, either. What could that mean for me? Also, had Bethany seen the kid in her dreams too? I decided I would ask her about him, no matter how crazy it sounded.

The walk to Bethany's door was always a quest. She lived in the exact center of a long building with half a dozen ID-activated doors between the main entrance and her room. Bethany, ever the gregarious social butterfly, often spent the better part of an hour getting to her room once she had entered the building because she would visit with everyone along the way. But we had no time for that.

Thea grabbed an unsuspecting student who had wandered outside for a smoke break and instructed him to take us to our destination. When he tried to ask questions, Thea narrowed her eyes, repeated her request, and that was the end of the conversation.

Like a knight unsheathing his sword, the smoker retrieved his ID with a bit of a flourish, and the obstacles of the locked doors were vanquished with a tap-and-beep. I slowed down as we got closer to Bethany's door because the weight of dread had found its way into the bottom of my feet. Thea, undeterred, shoved past me and banged on the door.

"Bethany! Bethany! Please open the door!" She waited a beat before adding, "NOW!" My skin seemed to all jump to the base of my neck. Thea was a force to be reckoned with, and if I were Bethany, I would be crawling through the underbrush of whatever ailment had me decommissioned to open that door. But she didn't answer. By Thea's third—very loud—attempt a crowd had gathered. I started canvassing everyone, asking if they had seen Bethany that day or the day before. No one had. Thea took off to find the dorm security guard, and I stared at the door, willing it to open. Willing Bethany to be ok on the other side of it. The crowd in the hallway began to grow larger, and with each unanswered knock, I thought my nerves would jump out of my skin and slither on down the hallway like escaped snakes. I couldn't wait for Thea to come back with the security guard.

As I liked to remind anyone who would listen, I spent my junior year of college in Barcelona. The lock to my apartment was always getting jammed, and in spite of many requests, the super never quite got around to fixing it. Eventually, my enterprising German roommate figured out that the most foolproof way to unlock the door was by using bobby pins. We joked that she led a secret life as a spy. That memory felt like an eternity ago.

While I hadn't had to grapple with a jammed lock in over half a decade, the habit of wearing bobby pins had stuck. I pulled one from my hair, unfolded it, and got to work on the lock. It took longer than usual, as my hands couldn't quite keep from coating themselves in an unhelpful layer of sweat. Finally, that telltale metallic click told me that the door was unlocked. I opened it a crack, called out for Bethany, and then pushed it open all the way.

The first thing I noticed was the smell. It slid up my nostrils and collided with my brain. Even still, it took a moment for it to light up circuits of recognition. Blood. I smelled it before I saw it—a purplish pool of coagulated blood on the floor. And on top of it was Bethany, her throat slit in a deep well that seemed to have stopped pumping several hours earlier.

The rest of that day was a series of still images as if my brain were taking photographs. A blue collar belonging to a police officer. The beige carpeting on the floor of the dorm lobby where we sat. Thea sitting next to me, stone-faced and stoic, answering questions because I had also turned into a photograph, and photographs don't speak. A blanket found its way over my shoulders, and I was escorted to the student health center. I couldn't stop shivering. My teeth kept chattering. The same sound from my dream. The sound that kid—

"Anna? Can you hear me?" The nurse buzzed around me, taking my vitals and shining a light in my eyes. I nodded. "You've had quite a shock today, and I am so sorry for your loss. I'm going to write a prescription for a little something to help you sleep."

Jesus. I should start selling the pills everyone is shoving down my throat to offset my tuition costs.

She continued. "I'm also going to put you in touch with one of our therapists who is available to see you tomorrow morning. For now, I want you to go home and get some rest."

The pain I started to feel in my pinky was the first sign that I was returning to my senses. Once again, I nodded. Danza and Mira were in the waiting room, and both of them had red, swollen faces—the aftermath of crying. They informed me of their intentions to escort me home, and walked with me between them, holding me up. Along the way, they granted me the gift of silence.

The leaves crunching underfoot as we walked through Harvard Yard were amplified in my ears, like the sound of hundreds of tiny bones snapping. The autumnal colors seemed to be muted in a hazy gray. Except for a burst of powder blue out of the corner of my eye. The kid from my dream was there on the other side of the Yard. I stopped walking and looked. A student passed in front of him and he was gone.

"What is it?" Danza asked. I shook my head. Somehow, we made it the rest of the way to my apartment. My friends tucked me in, fed me my pill, and I was asleep before the door had closed behind them.

Once again, my sleep was mercifully dreamless.

Bethany's death had been ruled a suicide. She had slit her own throat. Her family had insisted on a private service with no friends allowed. And so the group of us arranged our own memorial service on a bridge over The Charles River. We shared memories, read passages from books she loved, and sprinkled pink rose petals—her favorite—into the water. And then we headed to the bar to get good and drunk.

"Here's what I don't understand," Mira slurred after her fifth round of lemon drop shots, "listen up, guys, because I asked that badass lady cop some questions. You know the one. I think she was hitting on me. Ha!" Mira tipped from her stool, and

Elle and Eden righted her again. "Anyway, she told me about the knife. Bomb, you probably don't remember the knife, because you were–," she pantomimed drawing circles in the air by her temple, the universal symbol for crazy, "but it was one she had gotten for her boyfriend before she moved out here. The handle was made of pearl or some shit, and she was all proud of it." She took a thoughtful sip of water which Eden had told her was vodka. She didn't seem to notice the difference. "And I recognized the knife when I was talking to the lady cop. But here's the thing. The thing is, I know that she didn't have that knife here. That knife was in California with her weird knife collecting boyfriend."

"How do you know?" Elle asked.

"Because I follow him on Instagram, and he posted some artsy picture of his knives after cleaning all of them last week. And guess what? That knife was there. In California." She pointed westward and took another swig of water. "So how, HOW, did it get all the way to fucking Massachusetts? Riddle me that."

"Are you serious? Or just drunk?" I heard someone ask.

"I'm both."

We all looked at each other, not sure how much stock to put in her at that particular moment. There could be any number of explanations for why and how the knife got to Massachusetts. If Bethany had truly been suicidal, she would have found a way to orchestrate her own demise. But I didn't believe for a moment that she had been suicidal. Just like I knew that my injured finger was not the result of a sleepwalking accident.

I took a sip of wine, but it felt wrong when it hit my stomach and made my gag reflex dance. I excused myself to go to the bathroom and instead left the bar, paying my tab on the way out. I knew my friends would never let me leave without bombarding me with questions about my mental well-being, especially considering everything we had been through over the past few days, and I simply didn't have the bandwidth in that moment. I was agitated to the point of physical discomfort—headache, nausea, a flu of terrible feelings. I pulled my hood over my head and picked up my pace. I needed to get home.

"Did you see the kid too, Bethany?" I said to the air. She had felt the strange numbness in her throat—and her throat had been slit—that I had felt in my fingers. *Numbness and blood.* I repeated the words like a mantra as I unlocked my apartment door. I needed more information.

The radiator's hiss greeted me as I opened the door, accompanied by a blast of heat. It hadn't been working properly for a few days and I had been too preoccupied to deal with it, so I got used to walking around in my bra and underwear. I left my clothes in a pile, walked to the card table that served as my kitchen table, and opened my laptop screen. A frantic feeling started to build in my chest as I began my research.

The telephone game originated in Japan, and according to the rules, if you fail to answer The Answer Man's questions, a hand will reach through the phone and tear off a body part. As the legend goes, The Answer Man had been born without a body or appendages and was simply a head. Tearing off the body parts of non-compliant players was the only way he could make himself feel complete. I didn't think it would be possible to survive with only a head, but then again, what exactly did I know? I was studying to be a linguist, not a doctor. I also didn't think it was possible for an apparition that we had summoned during a stupid game to murder someone or gnaw off my fingertip. But then again, what did I know? "Besides," I said to myself as I slammed my laptop shut, "how does The Answer Man reach through the phone with his hand if he doesn't even have one?" I knew I had him there, trapped by language and logic. I stood up and walked to the window, still in my underwear, not caring if a casual passerby happened to see. Joseph's light was off. Too bad. I didn't feel like being alone.

Nothing was making any sense. The kid I had seen in my dreams and in the Yard, the kid who I was beginning to think had injured my hand and slit Bethany's throat, wasn't disfigured, and he wasn't a man. And a disembodied hand had certainly not reached through the phone. But still...we had *communicated* with someone, and I kept seeing him. So, who or what was he, exactly? And, the part of both my body and Bethany's that had been numb had also been injured, which matched The Answer Man's M.O. But the other aspects didn't seem to fit the description from the Japanese game. So what, exactly, were we dealing with?

My fingers started tingling again. "What is it you're trying to tell me?" I said to my hands. I pulled down all of the shades and sat back down at the table. The Internet had given me no information about how to stop The Answer Man, or whatever he was. It was too late for Bethany. But there had to be something I could do. I opened up my laptop again and started scouring the Internet for information about a kid who had died in Cambridge a long time ago. I hopped onto some ghost forums to see if anyone had encountered this particular spirit of the dark-haired kid in a blue suit. While I found a ton of articles about dead children, none of the pictures or details seemed to match the boy I was seeing. Fruitless Internet searches were a rarity for me, and I found myself almost apoplectic as my research refused to yield information. I would have to figure out another way.

I knew sleep was not going to happen for me that night, so I figured I might as well brew some coffee and get a jump start on a paper that was due later that week. My friends and I had been given a bereavement week and were excused from our classes and assignments, but I needed something to keep my mind busy, and my numb, tingling fingers moving. I worked until it was time to go to class.

I wasn't surprised to see Thea in class as well. Other than Bethany, she was the most steadfast and reliable person I knew. The rest of our friends were most likely too hungover and sad, and therefore did the sensible thing and stayed in bed. I was worried she would send me on a guilt trip about my abrupt exit the night before, but thankfully she just nodded a greeting and we busied ourselves with the task of pulling out our materials. The professor of this class was much less interesting to look at than our favorite one, though her bright, perky voice would definitely keep me awake.

We were halfway through a lecture on the monitor hypothesis when my eyes drifted to the window. Our classroom looked out onto Radcliffe Yard – the former little sister to Harvard's strapping big brother – where students were walking between classes, hunched over textbooks, and stress smoking.

The kid in the blue suit was standing in the middle of it all, staring at me.

I closed my eyes and shook my head in an attempt to clear his image the same way I would an Etch-A-Sketch. When I looked again, he was gone. The lack of sleep was catching up to me. I focused on taking notes as my professor's voice twittered on. I had never noticed how soft and melodic her voice really was. Almost soothing....

Stay focused. Stay awake.

"Krashen's work on the affective filter further demonstrates the link between language acquisition and emotional states...."

Stay focused. Krashen. Affective filter. Soothing voice...kid in the blue suit standing in front of me....

"WHAT ARE THE SINS OF YOUR FATHER?"

I screamed in response.

Everyone looked at me. I had screamed in the middle of class. This was a moment out of an actual

146

nightmare, except I wasn't in my underwear.

The kid was gone. But he had been there, right in front of me.

"Anna?" My professor looked shocked and concerned, and I couldn't bear seeing that expression on her face. I could feel Thea staring. Everyone was staring. Wordlessly I gathered my materials and ran out of the room. I shoved everything into my messenger bag and slung it over my shoulder, picking up speed as I did.

I could feel him watching me. I kept my eyes straight ahead, worried that if I turned around or looked anywhere else, I would see him. My nerves turned icy, crackling under my skin with the primal knowing that something was chasing me. The usual hubbub of Harvard Yard seemed menacing as I ran through it. The curious glances I drew as I flailed my way home seemed predatory as if they would be accompanied by a gnashing of teeth and a puncturing of my jugular. I ran, weaving in and out of students, bumping against tourists, raising my messenger bag in its familiar battering ram position. But I couldn't outrun him.

First, I heard his teeth chatter. And then, he was right in front of me. He grabbed my hand, brought it to his mouth, and everything went black.

When I woke up a halo of concerned faces was hovering over me, and I was bleeding. This time, from the index finger on my left hand. I was more embarrassed than frightened or in pain. Also, frustrated. *Jesus Hank Christ on a cracker. I'm going to have to go back to the infirmary AGAIN.*

And I did. This time I was interviewed by a

campus social worker who commented on my matching finger injuries—both of them significant enough to require stitches, and neither with any clear cause that I could remember. I blamed stress, grief, exhaustion, dehydration, and doing weird things in my sleep. They sent me home—this time with a prescription to help my anxiety—and I slept for the next 24 hours. Once again, the sleep was dreamless.

While horror movies were definitely not my favorite, and I really only watched them if I had been overruled in the movie selection process by whoever my movie night companion might be, I had seen enough to know that there was usually a scene in a musty library basement, during which the protagonist digs through files of papers browned with age, or scrolls through rolls and rolls of microfiche until finally arriving at an "aha" moment about whatever spirit might be plaguing her. It occurred to me after a night of rest—I had slept more in the past month than I had in the past year combined—that maybe the kid I was seeing wasn't The Answer Man that was dreamed up by some Japanese teenagers. Maybe it was a local ghost who had a similar penchant for questions and vengeance. If the Internet couldn't help me, maybe the archives could. I figured it was worth a try. After all, as hard as it is to believe, not every single newspaper article from every local rag dating back until forever could be found online. Some information was still stored in analog. And I was determined to find it.

Widener Library sits like royalty in the middle

of Harvard Yard, and I always felt a haughty sense of self-importance as I walked up its multitude of stairs and between its pillars. The microfiche was not, to my dismay, located in a basement. Rather, it was situated in the corner of a reading room with high ceilings and classic green lamps on each table.

"Let's see," I said to myself as I sat in front of the prehistoric behemoth of a machine, just before I was shushed by an overzealous librarian. *The kid I have been seeing looks as if he was dressed for some kind of fancy event. And he looks like he was wearing clothing that was old-fashioned, but not too old-fashioned. Maybe I'll start in the 1920s?*

As it turns out, there's a reason why horror movies use the library scenes as an opportunity for a musical montage. Searching through newspaper articles that span several decades—especially when you are not quite sure what you are looking for—is tedious, boring work, and it took the better part of a week.

But finally, there he was.

Finn McCarthy, the ten-year-old son of Irish immigrant laborers, went missing after church in the spring of 1939. He was never found. But there he was, in a fuzzy photo, right there on the screen.

I leaned back in my chair, posing in my aha moment for the horror movie camera in my imagination. Maybe a stranger had lured him away from the church with a question—something that had seemed innocuous or even playful—while his family socialized with fellow congregants. Maybe he asked his captor over and over again when he would be released back to the safety of his family.

149

And maybe his family had been forced to live the rest of their days steeped in questions with no answers about what had happened to their beloved Finn.

I couldn't figure out how, exactly, the ghost of a child in Massachusetts had taken on the characteristics of a ghost from a Japanese game, but again, what did I know? Maybe spirits had their own text message communication system. Maybe Finn had been lurking around us, listening, and we gave him the idea. I couldn't explain it. But, then again, I couldn't explain anything that was happening. After some deep thinking, I did, however, figure out exactly what I needed to do to make it all stop. I picked up my phone and typed a group text.

"Thank you all for meeting me here. I'm sorry I was vague in my text." We were all gathered once again in front of John Harvard's statue, a few moments before midnight. Thea, Mira, Danza, Elle, Eden, and me. It felt strange without Bethany. There were not ten of us, like the exact number of participants we had had the first time we played the game, but I knew he'd take my call.

"You said you had information about Bethany's death? What's going on, Anna?" Thea's eyes narrowed. I could hear side conversations starting and I raised my uninjured hand to silence them.

"Listen, when we played the telephone game that night, I don't think Bethany answered Finn's— er, The Answer Man's question. And ever since that night, strange things have been happening."

Everyone averted their eyes. Clearly, they had all heard about my screaming episode during class and were embarrassed for me. I wished that embarrassment had been my overriding feeling in that moment. I raised my bandaged hand and pointed to it. "The Answer Man is doing this to me. Except it's not like the one in the game that Bethany thought she was talking to. It's the ghost of a kid who went missing." I took a breath. I knew they'd have questions, but I had to keep going. "And it's this ghost that is doing this to me. And it's because of this ghost that Bethany is dead."

"What is going on with you, Anna? First, you completely freak out and self-harm and take enough sleeping pills to kill a small elephant, and now you are talking about some missing kid?" Danza was usually the patient one, but even she had her limits.

"There's only one way to make this right," I said, looking down. "We have to play the game again."

"Oh, fuck no, are you crazy!" Mira stood and threw up her hands. "Bethany's dead! Is this a joke to you? You are cracking up. The only number we should be calling is your therapist." She began striding away from the circle with Elle and Eden following behind.

"Stop. Wait. This isn't a joke. And if we don't do this, I will be the next one to die."

Mira slowly turned back to me. "What are you talking about?"

"Bethany didn't answer the question she was asked. And I...didn't either. I didn't either, ok?" I could feel myself becoming preemptively defensive as I anticipated their reactions. "He asked me a question that I couldn't bring myself to answer in front of you guys. I fucked up, ok?" Mira stood her ground. She didn't rejoin the circle, but she didn't leave either. I continued my plea. "The only way for me to fix this is to play the game again. And this time, I have to answer his question."

Mira, Elle, and Eden all exchanged glances. Mira nodded slightly and the three of them returned to the circle. Once again, we readied ourselves to call the person to our left. The drunken anticipation and adrenaline rush of our first time playing the game was no longer present. The feelings of anger and sadness and fear were palpable around the circle. On my countdown, we all clicked our call buttons.

Once again, I heard static, some wheezing, and teeth chattering. I waited. After a few moments, the question finally came one more time. But this time I was ready to answer.

"What are the sins of my father? Here they are. He was a math teacher at a prominent private high school in New York, and he had an affair with two of his female students. They were sixteen. A year younger than I had been at the time." I swallowed hard and kept my eyes on the ground directly in front of me. "My father was charged with child endangerment and criminal sexual misconduct. That is his sin. He's been in prison for ten years, and will be there for another ten." I took a breath and willed my gag reflex to stay still. "He's a fucking pedophile. He's disgusting. My mom, sister, and I took my mother's maiden name and moved to the

Midwest to distance ourselves from him. We are done with him, and he can rot in hell for all I care." My breath became elusive. I crouched in the perfectly groomed Harvard Yard grass and kept the phone pressed against my ear, waiting for a response, but none came. I closed my eyes and drew my last reserves of breath. "The sins of the father are NOT the sins of the daughter. I am nothing like my father. Nothing at all. And I never will be. So stop punishing me. I'm sorry that you died young, and terrible things must have happened to you by someone who preyed on you the way my father preyed on his students. But that is not my fault. So leave me the FUCK ALONE!"

I waited, suppressing my desire to cry. He didn't deserve my tears. Neither did my father. I heard teeth chattering on the other end of the phone, followed by static. And then the call went dead. Finn was gone.

I couldn't look at my friends. I needed to get out of there. Somehow my body was able to unfurl itself from its crouched position, and my legs could still carry me in the direction of my apartment. But I was stopped by an arm slung across my shoulders. First one, then two, and then the entire circle had converged. A dozen arms were locked around me, holding me up. My friends. They were all there. Every single one of them. Their slender arms made a surprisingly strong column around me. Nothing— human or supernatural—could hurt me.

Before I could stop myself, I was howling like a wolf, releasing the filthy feelings I had carried for a decade. They escaped from my mouth like ghosts.

And still, the column remained unwavering around me. Once the chamber of my body was empty of its unwelcome inhabitants, my tears stopped and my breathing returned back to normal. We all stood in a solemn, loving silence.

But only for a moment. "Who needs a scorpion bowl?" Mira said. We disentangled ourselves from each other with a laugh and made a beeline for The Hong Kong and its signature drink: a fruit-flavored, overly-sweet concoction dripping with plastic animals that was deadly in its potency. I felt gloriously empty. I would enjoy filling this newfound canyon inside of me with joy and alcohol. Not necessarily in that order.

A few nights later I saw Joseph for the first time in over a month. He had been traveling and working a lot, apparently. He had cradled my bandaged hand in his when I first saw him and I melted.

"What happened?"

"Cooking-related accident. I was attempting a complicated soufflé and nearly cut all of my fingers off. I'm not allowed to cook. Doctor's orders." He pulled me into a hug and I nestled my head into his chest. I was happy.

For the next two weeks, Joseph and I alternated in a repeating cycle of working, eating, snuggling, and having sex. While I knew my friends didn't approve of him, they still mostly kept their thoughts to themselves. Our message threads meandered back to ridiculous topics and jokes, and everything felt light. We still grieved for Bethany. We always would.

Spring came, graduation loomed, and the security of my friendships and relationship became further cemented. Joseph and I made cohabitation plans. I decided to spend the next year working and preparing to return for a doctorate degree, and though the rest of my friends would be scattered beyond Cambridge, Skype and email would keep us together. So would our sentimental mix CDs that we had gotten in the habit of making for each other.

Six months after our final scorpion bowl and tearful goodbyes, my friends went off to new adventures, and Joseph and I had settled into life in his bachelor pad. It felt strange and exciting to be on the other side of the windows I had monitored so closely from my old apartment. I began to work with equanimity on transforming Joseph's man cave into a comfortable space for the two of us, and a space more befitting a Harvard professor, as he seemed to be perpetually in college mode. I replaced the thumb-tacked posters with framed prints, threw out the forest of dead plants on the windowsills, and moved the beanbag chairs to the back corner of a closet. I waited patiently for the diamond that I knew was coming, dropping not-so-subtle hints about cut and carats regularly. I would worry about the betrayal later. Or maybe I wouldn't worry about it at all.

One night, Joseph and I had settled into our nightly ritual of spooning on the living room futon—a piece of furniture I couldn't quite convince him to replace with an actual couch—and watching old action movies. I succumbed to exhaustion and followed my usual pattern of turning toward him, throwing my leg over his hip, and falling asleep until he escorted me to bed.

That night I woke up at 3 a.m. after a terrible dream. Joseph was snoring loudly next to me and I knew it would be hard to get back to sleep with the cacophony on the other side of the bed, and so it was a perfect time for a cup of tea. I walked down the hallway from our bedroom, through the living room, and into the kitchen, where I popped a mug of water into the microwave and pulled out a packet of sleepytime tea. As it steeped, I heard something. Chattering. I brushed it away before recognition could set in. Before it could activate my adrenal glands and set the fear to work throughout my body. But still…the sound was there.

I walked from the kitchen to the living room and flipped on the light. I could feel him before I saw him. He was in a corner of the room by the radiator, staring at me.

"No. You can't be here. You shouldn't be here. I answered your question. I don't know what more you want from me."

He stared. His teeth chattered. I waited for his response. I waited for my fear to fulfill its duty.

But some feeling other than fear started to fill the cavern in me that had been left empty the night that I had vanquished The Answer Man with my confession. Or so I had thought. Anger. Or, more specifically, indignance.

How dare you. You shouldn't be here. I made you go away. And now I've built this perfect life and you are here to scare me and shit all over it. No.

Not this time.

"I answered your question. You ate two of my fingertips and killed my friend. You," I pointed to the door, "need to leave. Now. You are not welcome here." I crossed my arms. And then, because I couldn't help myself: "And you can suck a dick."

He took a step toward me, his bloodshot eyes twinkling terribly in his bone-white face.

"No." I stomped my foot and put my hands on my hips. "Fuck you."

With a glance from him, I became paralyzed as if he had shot me in the jugular with a dart. And then, in another second, I was flat on my back. My eyes could move, and a whimper tried to claw its way out of my throat. But otherwise, I was immobile. Frozen. Staring at the cracked plaster ceiling, willing my limbs to move.

I could feel my fingertips. The numbness that had busied itself there now spread to the rest of my body and my fingertips could feel everything. I could feel it when his teeth clamped onto my finger—this time the ring finger on my left hand, the very one where Joseph would eventually place my diamond ring. My fingernail ripped softly, and with a yielding, juicy sound—not unlike the mango skins I peeled almost daily. But the viscous juice that flowed in the aftermath was not sweet and delectable. It was mine. And that finger stung in excruciating pain as exposed flesh met the cruel twinge of air. All I could do was lie there and take it as my fight or flight instincts threw themselves fruitlessly against my immobility.

When he was done the feeling slowly returned to my limbs, and I could blink and swallow as sensation returned to the various places it belonged, like a river returning to its deltas after a drought. When I could lift my head and look around, Finn—The Answer Man—was gone.

He had devoured three of my ten fingertips, and I knew he'd be back for the rest. Answering his question had done nothing to alter what was already set in motion. It had just caused me pain and embarrassment. It would have been comforting to know exactly when he would choose to appear in my life moving forward. But he was not going to do me that kindness. He wouldn't stop until he was done, and I would have to live with that uncertainty, and with the knowledge that there would be seven more nights like this. I was at the mercy of his whims.

That night I found myself wondering about the question that he had asked Bethany. Somehow the offense of her not answering his question had cost her her life. I would never know what the question was, or why it was so important. I would have thought that the secret I was carrying would have had a greater penance. I don't know. Maybe it's because I answered my question eventually that I was able to keep my life. Or maybe it was simply luck of the draw: Finn had chosen Bethany's throat as his target, and he had chosen my fingers. Maybe it was a complete act of randomness that decided who lived and who died. Perhaps if The Answer Man had chosen me first to answer the call, like he had chosen Bethany, I would no longer be alive. But

I was. The odds had been randomly stacked in my favor, minus some pain and scarring.

An odd picture popped into my head as I envisioned Finn standing in front of a rotating case of body parts—not unlike many a display case of pies I had known in my time. However, instead of picking the banana cream pie versus the cherry, he picked the fingers versus the throat. I didn't know. I'd never know.

The pain in my newly devoured fingertip set in. Luckily, I had paid attention to how the nurses had bandaged my two other fingers, and so I was able to replicate it with the first aid kit we kept in the medicine cabinet. I returned to the living room and sat down on Joseph's futon with my hand raised to curb the bleeding. I looked like a student waiting to answer a question. The irony was not lost on me.

I stayed that way until dawn started to infiltrate the curtains I had hung in an attempt to make the living room look softer and more feminine. Certain things began to dawn on me as well. If The Answer Man was right, a life with Joseph would come with a price. He would betray me. But, hadn't I overcome a worse betrayal from my father? Would Joseph's future mistake be worth upending the first touchstone of stability I had experienced in a decade?

The sins of the daughter might not be the sins of the father, but I was linked to them nonetheless. I could never escape what my father had done. It would stain my inner world forever, and the scars on my fingers would provide daily reminders that The Answer Man was punishing me for my father's sins. My wounds would heal, but my fingers would never be the same as they were before I played that game. Maybe complete healing is impossible. Maybe there is no such thing as redemption, even after our debt has been paid. The Answer Man would not stop until I had completed my penance and he had devoured all ten of my fingertips. And maybe that would not be enough to stop him even then. A vengeful appetite can never be sated.

I changed my bandages again and crawled back in bed next to Joseph. I thought about Bethany. I mourned her again for the first time in over a year. Maybe her mistake had allowed me to live. I wish I had known what painful secret she was carrying. But I never would.

I still had almost an hour before my alarm was set to go off. Joseph stopped snoring for a moment, and, half-asleep, reached out and reassuringly rubbed my back. I grinned. Whatever his mistakes may be, I knew I could forge ahead with him.

Perhaps it was my lot in life to love deceitful men but be bolstered by infallible women. Maybe I would never fully be able to trust the man who would eventually become my husband. But I would always trust my friends to get me through anything. Even the next attacks by The Answer Man – whenever they would be. He had total control. All I could do was wait, heal, and wait again. And he would be watching until he was finished with me.

The Bathtub Game

I wasn't always like this. Boring. Out of shape. My identity wasn't always shackled to three others—my husband and two adolescents. I feel myself dissolving further and further into them each day, and the layers of the life I had before peel away like snakeskin. My Ivy League education. The two years I spent traveling. My career as an interior designer. My spirituality. They are all disappearing. The hum of colleagues in an office space has been replaced with shouting. So much shouting, all day long. It's a circular beast, feeding on its own tail. My son yells at my daughter. My daughter yells at my husband. My husband yells at me. I yell at my son. And on and on until we are devoured by the din of our own voices. Spent.

Words like *depression* and *anxiety* are bandied about so often these days as an explanation for every single woe, nervous thought, or temporary malaise one might have. The seriousness of them seems to have faded with overuse. What my psychiatrist diagnosed as depression, some people in my life call "laziness." And they call my clinical anxiety, "being a drama queen." Over the years, both of these diseases have spread further and deeper into my life like unchecked water damage.

Years ago, I had used my interior design talents to sculpt and mold our home—our stunning, post-modern home built into the side of a mountain with the outward-facing side covered in glass—and it is perfection. Not to mention the fact that we own the mountain, if there is such a thing as being able to "own a mountain." The house fortifies me. I designed it meticulously out of reclaimed wood, adorned it with original art, and lined it with feather beds. The exterior is perfectly symmetrical, and the interior is covered in serene shades of white and off-white whose paint names sound like decadent desserts. And on the other side of the glass walls, there are mountains beyond mountains, with their snow-capped peaks also coated in white. There are cozy spaces, a plethora of pillows and blankets, and color-coordinated storage. The master bedroom, kitchen, and living room are upstairs, and the kids' bedrooms and family room are downstairs. My kids have full ownership over their rooms, but luckily, they have both inherited my sense of style: a desire for clean lines, minimal clutter, and cozy materials. Yes, the house is my magnum opus. But it is also a daily reminder of my wasted talents.

Late morning is always my least favorite time of day, and this day was no different. The kids were off to school, my husband was off to work, and I had just finished the breakfast cleanup. There I was, standing at the top of the stairs, looking out over the mountains like I did every weekday morning. Time was stretching in front of me in endless ribbons, unfurling to nowhere. Between work, sports, and social engagements, no one but me would be home until evening. I decided I might as well change into yoga clothes and try to make a workout happen at some point that day. I released my long black hair from its nest on top of my head, combed it, and put it back into a marginally neater topknot. I didn't bother with make-up. So much about my face changed after turning 40 over three years ago, but my blue eyes had still somehow escaped the signs of aging that had insinuated themselves across the rest of my face. Most notably, the wrinkles. Goodness gracious, the wrinkles. My husband had suggested Botox on many occasions, but somehow the inability to make facial expressions seemed like a worse tradeoff. My facial expressions felt like one of the few remaining ways in which I could, well, express myself. I would not relinquish that power.

"Her hair was black and her eyes were blue." It was a line from a song called "Galway Girl," and my future husband sang it to me on a rainy night in where else but Galway, when we first met. We were both spending our junior year of college abroad in Ireland. I had a long-distance boyfriend back in the US, and my future husband nursed a crush on me the entire time. Nothing would happen until three years later when he sought me out over social media. A part of him had been holding a vigil that entire time, waiting for me like a crystal glass protecting a flame. It was a flame that I still saw now, just barely, dancing in the back of his eyes— after the kids were asleep, and the kitchen was clean, and the bills were paid. Then, we would find each other once again and strip down to the tender beings that we had been before the years had accumulated over them. Those moments, however, were fewer and farther between.

I hummed "Galway Girl" to myself and decided that what I needed that morning was a stroll down memory lane, as it were. Time to reflect, remember, and reconnect with the spaces inside of me that were mine alone. I descended the stairs, walked past the kids' bedrooms, and entered the walk-in linen closet at the end of the hallway. On the third shelf from the top, I kept my great-grandmother's monogrammed linen napkins, a wedding gift given to her many decades ago, which I would never use for company, as time had made them brittle. Behind the napkins was a removable panel in the wall.

"Well. Hello, there." One benefit of overseeing the design and build of our home was the decision to install a secret compartment for my most treasured memories and heirlooms—the things that were just for me, that I did not want to be touched by others. I pulled them out one by one and gingerly placed them on the hallway carpet, taking stock of them all: there was the letter sent to me by Princess Diana's lady-in-waiting in response to a letter I had written to her; a small, mahogany box containing my grandmother's spoon collection; another box containing her porcelain Christmas ornaments; a glass jar filled with my baby teeth; and, of course, my many volumes of diaries that I had kept since the age of nine. The items at the very back, the ones I had hidden the most deeply, stirred dusty corners of my brain that had been uninhabited for decades: my silver pentagram, several quartz crystals, and a healing stick made especially for me by the Official Witch of Salem. I had grown up two hours from Salem and made my yearly pilgrimage there starting at the age of 13. By that time, the site of historic atrocities (which, of course, had everything to do with greed and power and nothing to do with actual witchcraft) had become a tourist trap filled with new age bookstores, Tarot card readers with fake accents, and zombie parades. But it didn't matter to me. Perhaps it was the collectively magical zeitgeist that was engendered there as a backlash of mass hysteria and essentially murder. Perhaps the soil was particularly nurturing for misfits and had a healing magnetic quality. Or perhaps the advertising was just too convincing. Regardless of the initial inspiration, Salem felt like a spiritual home for me – especially in October.

The Official Witch of Salem owns a shop named Crow Haven Corner, and the first time I visited her shop, I fainted. I told myself it was a result of the energy of the store completely overwhelming me. Indeed, it was a sign that Wicca was meant to be my spiritual path. Doctors later told me it was a result of low blood pressure and dehydration (which would become a chronic problem for me. Which means that hot baths are not good for me. Which means I should know better than to take them. And yet, they remain a frequent indulgence). In any case, The Official Witch herself happened to be in residence that day, and as her employees revived me with water, an invigorating scent, and a sacred bird feather, she emerged from her back room—floating, if my delirious brain correctly recalls, in dark scarves with her feet not quite touching the ground—and handed me a healing stick carved from a piece of cedar that she had found while walking in a sacred forest.

"Here." That was the only word she spoke. It

was the only one she needed to speak. It was carved to resemble an old man with a beard that tapered to one end of the stick. Above the other end was a perfectly clear ball of quartz. It vibrated in my hands like an out-of-control tuning fork, matching my already frenetic vibration. And I instantly felt better. As quickly as she had come, she was gone. And her employees knew that they did not need to call an ambulance. They also somehow knew to sell me another $100 worth of merchandise, but I digress.

It was so strange because in that vulnerable moment, I felt cared for. I felt seen. And it was the start of a spiritual path for me. At least until I became too old and practical and jaded.

The healing stick had been wrapped in a handkerchief given to me by the high priestess of the Wiccan coven that I did eventually join during my senior year of high school. Unbeknownst to all of my friends and teachers. I was the Princeton-bound, stellar athlete. No one needed to know that I was performing rituals at each full moon, and developing my own psychic abilities to divine the future. Though no one knew it, it was the happiest and (literally) most magical time of my entire life.

Well, there was one person who knew. Sort of. She at least had a healthy glimpse into my life as a teenage witch. And it only brought us closer.

Her name was Anne, and we were so inseparable that classmates and family members made a portmanteau word out of our names: "Morgan" and "Anne" simply became "MorGANNE." We met while pursuing one of our shared interests—horseback riding, but our friendship initially flourished over detailed conversations about our main shared interest: boys. However, it was through discovering that we shared a unique characteristic that our bond was cemented.

The first time Anne slept over at my house, we were sitting on my floor looking through a collection of horse magazines when we heard someone walk down the long hallway to my bedroom and pause for a moment outside of my door. Then, ever so slowly, the door creaked open.

No one was there.

Anne had turned around to face the door, and when she faced me again her eyes were wide.

"Sorry," I said sheepishly. "I think I live in a haunted house."

A look of relief spread over her face. "Thank goodness!" she said. I looked at her sideways. "I think I live in one, too!"

Our sleepovers became ghost adventures unto themselves as we alternated between the rather harmless and kindly ghosts of my house, and the more aggressive ones at hers. At her house, lights would flicker, mirrors would shatter, and there was the occasional unexplained kitchen fire. Growing up in these environments seemed to prime our psychic abilities. I would later discover that I had the power of premonition dreams. Through my dreams, I could tell the future. Anne had discovered that she was a psychometrist, or "touch-know." She could touch an object and see its history.

After having multiple premonition dreams about death, I vehemently prayed and begged the

Universe to take this ability from me. It was too much of a burden for my teenage self to bear. Not only did I stop having the dreams, but all of my abilities and contact with the supernatural stopped. I could no longer see ghosts or communicate with spirits. My spells stopped working. Even the intricate vibrations of crystals that I could feel in my palms as if they were living things with heartbeats thrumming like those of baby birds, became still. The crystals were simply cold, smooth stones, completely indistinguishable from one another. I was devastated. The abilities and experiences which outlined my very identity, and upon which I hung my understanding of myself and the world, were just gone. I became a shapeless cloud of vapor misting my way through my own existence, and it was difficult to find the meaning in it all.

Eventually, Anne and I finished high school and went to college in separate states, and the tethers that had bound us to one another—the supernatural and horses—abruptly snapped. I could no longer connect with the supernatural, and Anne could no longer afford to ride horses. And so, we drifted away from each other, as friends sometimes do.

I spread the journals out on the floor, inspecting their covers until I found the one that I was looking for. This was the journal that documented my friendship with Anne, my record of spells and rituals, and the assorted deep yearnings of a teenager whose hope in the world had yet to be dismantled. A sharp knot punched its way up my throat as a dreadful thought that I had kept in the walled-off back part of my brain finally broke through: the time described in the pages of that journal had been the last time that I was truly happy.

The journal was black, naturally, and adorned with the saying, "Life is too short to drink cheap wine." Part of what had made this axiomatic sentence humorous to me at the time was that I had been a self-proclaimed teenage teetotaler. While my friends binged on beer, I sipped black cherry seltzer.

I put away my treasures, replaced the panel and napkins, and tucked the diary under my arm. I felt mischievous—the way I imagined a teenage boy with a dirty magazine would feel. I would revisit my happiest time and all the delicious secrets that I had kept during it.

I decided that morning to indulge in another wildly decadent activity: taking a bath. Wicca had instilled in me a deep reverence for the structure of rituals, and though my Wiccan membership had been revoked by the Powers That Be, I still tried to make as many tasks in life as possible into a ritual. Bath time was no exception. Its steps brought me a serenity rarely found in the rest of my day: First, you rinse out the tub with three glassfuls of water and allow it to drain. The next part is like crafting a potion: you dump in the perfect combination of salts, bubble bath, and aromatherapy. After that, you dim the lights, ignite some scented candles, and put your robe and slippers in just right spot where they are easily accessible but will still stay dry. No books. No magazines. You just let your thoughts roll around in that dark cavern of your mind. Today, though, I would make an exception and read that journal.

The water was warm and smelled nurturing, and revisiting my old words made my eyes instantly well up. That insecure scrawl of my handwriting, that desire to be loved and understood, and that gang of friends running around like nerdy misfits. It described joy flavored with a hint of painful self-criticism. My hand spewed poetry across the pages, as natural to me as breathing. As I read it, I realized that I didn't recall the exact day that the poetry stopped. But one day, it did. The now hot stream of tears began to mingle with the steam from the tub, and I had to keep wiping my eyes in order to see. Those feelings of becoming, anticipating what the future would be, waiting to be a grown-up while also dreading it, the pain and creativity and self-immolation…I simultaneously grieved my 17-year-old self and brought her back to life. And I relished it.

On the back cover of the journal, I had taped a folded sheet of paper. I had written, "try this with Anne?" across the front, and long since forgotten its contents. The tape had turned useless with age, and after pulling off the paper I carefully unfolded it, scared that it would crumble into dust. More of my handwriting was scrawled across the paper. Strange. I didn't remember writing any of it. It read:

The Bathtub Game—from Japan
Warning: THIS GAME IS VERY DANGEROUS. Follow the instructions EXACTLY as they are written, NO MATTER WHAT. Bad

things will happen if you do not. This game is intended to summon the spirit of a woman who fell in a bathtub and died.

Well. This was not sounding at all safe or promising. I continued reading:

Wait until night. Draw a bath. Wash your hair, while repeating the words "Daruma-san fell down," over and over. Envision a Japanese woman standing in the tub. She slips and falls onto a rusty tap. The tap goes through her eye and kills her. You may hear or feel a slight movement in the water behind you. Keep your eyes closed. You have summoned a ghost.

I skimmed the rest. A ghostly figure with long, black hair and only one eye will rise out of the water behind you. She will follow you wherever you go. Whenever you turn to look, she will disappear. When you glance over your shoulder, you will catch a glimpse of her. Though she may draw closer as the day goes on, do not allow her to catch you. To end the game, you must look at her and shout, *Kitta!,* which means, *I cut you loose!* Hold out your hand and swing it in a cutting motion.

I wondered why I had taped the instructions in my journal instead of playing the game with Anne. My best guess was that I had come across it in the "after" part of my spiritual and psychic journey, and the "after" part of my friendship with Anne. I maybe hoped for a moment that it would once again put me in touch with the spirit world, and with my friend, but it was an idea I clearly hadn't entertained for very long. And so I had taped it in my journal as an afterthought.

I shifted in the tub, sending waves outward. I had gotten the water temperature just right, and I could have stayed there all day. As I contemplated the instructions I had just read, a grin spread across my face. I set the paper on the edge of the tub and grabbed the antique silver hand mirror from its spot on the windowsill—a gift from my grandmother that was not discarded in my minimalist rampage because it looked so charming with the other lovely products that were staged by the tub—and looked at my reflection. Really looked at it. Usually, I did the "glance and groan," in which I looked at myself just long enough to apply makeup while releasing an audible groan at the signs of aging that spelled themselves across my face. But there in the tub, I looked at myself thoroughly, for the first time in years. I hated my under-eye bags, and the traces of the speckled age spots that I treated monthly with lasers. But...I was pretty. My skin had fine lines, but it was taut, and my cheekbones carved definition into my face. And, of course, there were my eyes – a feature that still continued to meet my approval. Admiring myself wasn't something I had done in far too long. I had always thought of myself as "formerly beautiful." But maybe that wasn't true. Maybe I wasn't just a wife or a mom. Maybe I was a beautiful woman. Still.

I set down the mirror and continued reading from my journal. As I flipped the pages, taking great care to not get them wet, I was suddenly back there once again. I could feel what it was like to sprawl out on my floral bedspread, listen to Nirvana's Unplugged album, and write with abandon. There was no censoring, no worrying about style or appearances, no pretense. Just freedom. It was blissful spending time reliving these memories—pulling them out, polishing them up, and examining them—just like I did once a year with my grandmother's spoon collection.

I finally reached the last pages of the journal, which documented the story that I had been equal parts excited to read and dreading: my final paranormal adventure with Anne. We had been exploring in the woods around my house—or, more specifically, the shed in the woods. It had been locked by the previous owners. My parents didn't have the key, and they didn't concern themselves with it either, as our house had close to 20 rooms, and therefore plenty of storage. It had been appearing in my dreams at that point at least weekly. The dreams weren't long, but in them I was running to the shed, panting, while an unseen pursuer chased after me. In the pages of the journal, I expressed fear and concern, that something had perhaps happened there, and that there was some disturbed energy that needed our assistance. And so, I dragged Anne out there with me. It had been winter, and there was a thin, crusty layer of snow on the ground. The trees had been leafless, skeletal hands, reaching hopelessly upward, waiting.

We had tugged on the padlocks and doors, trying to find a way inside, but they were unyielding. There was nothing unusual about the shed itself or the area around it—or so we thought at first. When Anne had wandered a little ways away from the shed, she discovered several piles of stones that had been carefully arranged into what appeared to be cairns. There was a half dozen of them, ranging in size from just a few stones to about the height of my knee.

I had learned about cairns from my mother after she returned from a trip to Wales with my aunt. Cairns were used as monuments, burial sites, or in rituals. They seemed out of place back in that forest, and Anne had crouched down to examine them further. She studied them carefully before rubbing her hands together and placing them on the stones – invoking her psychic powers—and closing her eyes.

In the journal, I described how she had pulled her hands back as if the stones had electrocuted her. *Morgan, we need to get out of here*, she had said. *The energy is terrible. Someone was murdered in this spot.* We turned around and prepared to run, but she was there, the woman I had seen in my dreams—or rather, her ghost—waiting for us. She wore a long brown dress—the kind that kitchen maids had worn during the turn of the century. Right around the time when my house was built on that land. Her throat was a deep shade of purple. Bruises. She had been strangled. She had reached her arms out to us—a gesture that, upon later reflection, may not have signaled insidious intent, but we did not interpret it that way at the time—and we scrambled around her, moving as quickly as the scrubby, naked foliage and snow would allow. Anne had fallen a few paces behind me, and I had heard her scream. I couldn't bring myself to look back and accelerated steadily until reaching the groomed space of my backyard. Only then did I turn around to see Anne running, wide-eyed and wild, with the ghost right behind her. And then I screamed.

When she got to the boundary between the yard and the forest the ghost had reached out one more time before vanishing.

Something terrible had happened in that forest, and darkness inhabited it. I only went into those woods one more time. The day before we moved, when the forest had exploded into its self-assured summer verdancy, I brought out some rosemary— for remembrance—and planted it next to the cairns. I had felt her watch me go, but couldn't bring myself to turn around for one last look.

As terrifying as this memory was, it was also thrilling. I loved that comingling of fear and exhilaration. That feeling of being able to touch something bigger than what was right in front of me, and experience more than what could simply be perceived by my feeble human senses, had been joyful. Exquisite. Transcendent, even. I missed that feeling terribly.

Rituals demarcate beginnings and endings. Funerals, weddings, births…they have their own distinct set of colors, symbols, and alcoholic beverages. I decided that what I needed was a ritual. My 17-year-old-self had been awakened in my older bones, and I needed a special ceremony to commemorate this moment of unity between my younger self and current self. I needed to draw a clear line between the self that was aging and filled with dread and the self that had run through that forest filled with fear, certainly, but also life and joy.

I thought about the power of ritual while treating my elbows to a salt scrub exfoliation. I thought about the way I used to feel. And then I glanced at the paper on the edge of the tub. Maybe I could help this ghost in a way that I couldn't help the one in the forest. Even if I couldn't, just seeing a ghost again, even one in a bathtub, would allow me to submerge myself (pun intended…I could already feel my sense of humor returning) in feelings I hadn't known in decades.

I looked over the instructions one more time, attempting to commit them to memory. There was the emphatic warning at the top of the page: the rules MUST be followed. As a former Wiccan, I knew the importance of adhering to strict instructions during spells and rituals. For instance, it was always necessary to cast a protective circle the same way each and every time before doing any magic. And spells that were not followed to the letter simply didn't work. And this game was supposed to be played at night.

I looked out the window. It was late morning, and I had nothing but time at my disposal, and nothing to fill it with. It seemed almost ungrateful to waste it and wait until night. I wasn't sure what I would do with myself until night otherwise – a fact that made me feel an almost gouging sense of loneliness. I also wasn't sure how I would explain what exactly I was doing while playing the game –

or explain why a creepy Japanese ghost was following me everywhere – to my husband or children, who would be home by then. And, ultimately, I wasn't even entirely sure that the game would work, so what was the harm in starting a little early?

"Besides," I said to no one in particular, "I've already drawn a bath." I grabbed the expensive shampoo from the windowsill and started washing my hair with my eyes closed. "Daruma-san fell down. Daruma-san fell down…" I repeated, several more times. I then envisioned the poor woman slipping and falling, and heard the squish and crack as her eyeball and skull made contact with the tap. It made such a grotesque, almost cartoonish sound in my imagination that I had to suppress the urge to giggle.

I kept my eyes closed and waited. I didn't hear or sense anything, except for the relentless dripping of the sink faucet, which needed to be fixed. I proceeded.

"Why did you fall in the bath?" Once again, I heard and felt nothing. According to the ritual instructions, the player is then supposed to climb out of the tub, leave the bathroom, and shut the door—all with her eyes closed. Evidently, the creator of The Bathtub Game was not a woman in her 40s who had no interest in a falling-related injury. No way was I going to try and navigate the slippery marble floor with my eyes closed.

I opened my eyes, wrapped myself in my favorite fuzzy robe, drained the bathtub, and surveyed my surroundings. There were no one-eyed ghosts present.

"Hello?" I called to the empty house, not quite sure what I was expecting in response. When I heard nothing, I decided to go ahead and start the time-consuming task of blow-drying and brushing my sopping wet hair. It had tentacles and clung to everything like an octopus until I could tame it with heat. I liked to sing along to the tedious whirring of the hairdryer.

"This little light of mine. I'm gonna let it shine." Whirr. My scalp began to heat up. "This little light of mine. I'm gonna let it shiiiine." I hung my head upside down to dry the underside. "This little light of mine. I'm gonna let it shine." With one enthusiastic flip, I was upright, and my hair spilled down my back. My brush became my microphone as I dried the ends. "Let it shine, let it shine, let it…."

In the mirror behind me was a figure in black and white—white, translucent skin; white nightgown; one white eye; one black one; framed in a tangle of black hair—and for a second I heard a rattling sound before I fainted.

When I came to, I was still holding the hairdryer, though its cord had been yanked out of the wall. I brought my hand to my head to check for lumps. I had low blood pressure and a terrible habit of passing out after hot showers and baths when I was too dehydrated. Clearly, the bath, robe, and hairdryer had been formidable opponents in my quest to remain upright. Strange hallucinations before passing out were not uncommon either, which explained the phantom lady in the mirror. I shimmied out of my robe and crawled into the adjoining bedroom where a bottle of Evian was perched on my nightstand. After heaving myself into bed and draining the bottle, I started to feel a little better. There was a tender spot where I had landed on the left side of my head, and I knew it would form a goose-egg lump before long.

"Great. Just great." I let myself fall into a dreamless sleep for a half-hour. When I awoke, I threw on my most comfortable sweat suit—the one my husband said made me look like a welder, whatever that meant—and walked out into the kitchen in search of some frozen peas to take down the swelling. It had been a long time since I had fainted. I shuddered, thinking about the ghost who hadn't been so lucky. Unlike me, she hadn't been able to avoid the tap in the bathtub. "So…you had low blood pressure, too?" I said to the air. At least we had that in common.

Smell is the sense most connected to memory. And, for visual learners like me, the next closest sense was sight. Sound rooted itself the least strongly in my brain. As I stood in the kitchen sipping a big glass of water, I heard the sound I thought I had hallucinated emanating from the bathroom. I briefly entertained the idea that it was one of the many electronics in our house being quirky. Except I knew that sound all too well. Something in my memory began stirring. Something I had buried years ago.

I drained the rest of my water and mustered the courage to go and investigate. I walked from the kitchen to my bedroom and threw open our matching-and-delightfully-separate closets, checked under our California King bed, and even threw open dresser drawers for good measure. Of course, nothing was there. I turned and saw the full-length mirror on my closet door and, given the beautiful self-love moment I had had but a few moments earlier, decided to give my entire body a positive review. I bent one knee and put one hand on my hip—reliable cheats for executing the perfect picture—and let my eyes wander over my long hair, still-perky breasts, and wide-but-voluptuous hips. I played around with different poses—even contemplated taking a picture to post on social media accounts—until I saw her. I really, truly saw her.

She was soaking wet, and her hair was like rotting seaweed, dark and tangled and hanging haphazardly from her head. Her skin had an oversaturated quality like it had been gnawed at by water for decades. And then there were her eyes: one filled in blackness, and the other was blank and bloody, like a white marble caught in a net of red veins. Beneath the white eye was a bruise, varied in its shades of purple and black and blue.

I am not entirely sure how I managed to look for so long—long enough for the details of her image to be processed and stored in my memory. But I did. And she opened her mouth and made that rattling sound, and it snapped me back to a different time. Maybe sound embeds itself in memory better than I had thought. It was the same sound I had heard one time when I visited my grandmother. It was the day before I left for college, several states away. I sat by her bed, holding her hand while she slept, and her breath had clattered like a ball bearing knocking around a hollow cavern. It was a strange sound—almost inhuman, and yet painfully mortal. She passed away moments later, while I was still holding her hand, and my mother coolly explained that the sound I had heard was a death rattle. It was the sound of the body shutting down. It echoed in my ears for weeks. And here it was again, emanating from a ghost in the mirror.

I fainted again. It seemed to be the only reasonable thing to do to alleviate my overwhelmed memory and nervous system. This time I was able to aim my body toward the bed, which gave me a soft landing. I wasn't out for long. If I was going to keep passing out, this was going to be a very long day. I sat up slowly, perched on the edge of the bed, and looked around. To my relief, the ghost was gone, but she had left behind a set of wet footprints, which led to the bathroom. I chose not to follow them. However, I knew I had to do something to communicate with this spirit. Isn't this exactly what I wanted? To touch the supernatural, and possibly help a tortured spirit. And yet, somehow it didn't feel like I thought it would. *Maybe if I could just talk to her*, I thought, *I could possibly alleviate my fear and thereby increase my chance of remaining both upright and conscious. I could also, quite possibly, help her to move beyond her torment and pain and give herself an existence beyond that of being summoned by bored teenagers. And housewives.*

And, in the meantime, I could ameliorate the

sense of guilt that I hadn't realized I had been carrying since that day in the forest with Anne. Guilt that my fear had taken over and I hadn't helped that poor-but-completely-terrifying ghost.

I mean, I planted rosemary. Isn't that something?

No. I would do things differently this time. "Well, I would like to help you if I can. But you have to stop scaring the *crap* out of me." I waited, not quite sure what I was waiting for. A chat session on the edge of the bed? A wet, death-rattle-y hug? An impromptu, wine-fueled dance party in my living room? Something flashed across the constellation of my feelings for a brief moment: crippling loneliness. Maybe even a tortured spirit didn't want to hang out with me. Luckily it crashed and burned before it had a chance to sink in.

I left the bedroom and walked to the kitchen. I had gotten a chill and needed something warm to drink. I put the kettle on, waited for it to whistle, and then, just for the hell of it, poured two cups of tea. I sat down on a stool at the kitchen island and put the second cup next to me. Two cups made of delicate bone china—white, of course—with matching saucers. I watched the steam rise, trying to decipher any hidden messages when I heard the unmistakable sound of wet feet slapping against the wood floor behind me. I didn't want to turn around. In fact, I couldn't have if I tried, because I found myself unable to move. I tried to unlock my brain and tell myself that she was just a soul in need, reaching out, and there was nothing to fear. She came closer, and I think I halfway hoped that she would pull up the stool next to me and drink her tea. Instead, I felt a pair of icy wet hands on my shoulders. I convulsed, surprised at the contraction of my muscles. The cold and fear shook me into a cocktail of awful movement, and I lost all control of my own body. And again, the death rattle—her only access to language, apparently – filled my ears and tangled with my memories. It became too much. I let out a high-pitched scream that my voice hadn't made since I was a little girl. The second cup flew across the room and shattered against the white marble backsplash between the microwave and the stove.

"Stop!" I yelled. I didn't have time to be scared, because I was too worried about the backsplash. Marble soaks in everything. It bubbles and hisses when something doesn't agree with it, so I had to move across the room with Olympic speed, dishtowel in hand, to mop up the mess. So much for our friendly tea.

I threw away the shards of perfect china, wiped down the surfaces, and had the unshakeable feeling that I had let a rabid raccoon inside. I wanted to hop onto the counter to spare my feet from vermin. I was scared, really scared, but also creeped out. I almost anticipated a swarm of insects to invade and deposit their slimy larvae all over my immaculate kitchen. I breathed deeply, trying to calm myself, the exact way my yoga teacher had trained me. When that didn't work I opened a cupboard and took my Xanax from its hiding place—inside of a jar of a repellant nutritional supplement that no one else in my family would touch—and gulped it down while repeating my own made-up mantra.

She's only a ghost. She can't hurt you. She's only a ghost. She can't hurt you. You need to help her. Be the bigger person. You need to help her. She's only a ghost. She's only a ghost. She's only a ghost.

A moment later, I noticed the water. It was covering the kitchen floor and rushing towards the stairs like a runaway toddler who was about to divebomb them. I looked at the French doors between the kitchen and the bedroom. My perfect ivory plush carpet was soaked. There could only be one source: the bathtub. I pulled off my socks and trod slowly through the water from the kitchen, and paused at the doors. A short walk and a left turn would lead to another set of French doors that opened into the bathroom. I could hear the bathtub faucet running. My heart was pounding. I knew she'd be standing there, waiting for me. The image of the forest ghost reaching out to me flashed in my mind. I shook my head to clear that image and placed a hand against the doorframe so that I could brace myself in case I started to faint again.

As I felt the water pooling at my feet, I couldn't help but think that perhaps I had done something stupid by playing this game. This was not the forest ghost, and I was not 17. I was starting to think that this ghost wasn't just lonely and misunderstood and in need of some sympathetic company. What seemed to be more likely was that she was vengeful. And her rage was, for that day at least, directed at me. I took slow and steady steps, forcing myself forward, into the bedroom and across the soaking wet carpet. I steadied myself against the bed briefly before walking to the bathroom.

The room itself was empty, but the bathtub had overflowed completely. I turned off the water and sat at the edge of the tub, listening, feeling my pants getting wetter and wetter with freezing cold bathwater. My breath was coming quickly, and I had to breathe through my mouth. The yoga nose breathing would no longer suffice. My Xanax had not yet kicked in. I waited, wondering if I should speak. Wondering if she needed to hear that her death had been unfair. She had died too young, and that I understood that she was angry. I was no stranger to anger myself.

There was a hand on the back of my neck. It slammed my face into the faucet, right on the cheekbone, and I fell into the tub face-down. Someone was holding my head underwater. I panicked, strained, and tried to scream. Images of a life that hadn't belonged to me flashed under my eyelids. I saw her, before the fall. It hadn't been an accident, but she hadn't seen who had pushed her. She had been pretty. Young. Hopeful. I felt my struggle slowing, and my lungs emptying. And then, nothing.

"Why the hell are you in the bathtub?" The lights flicked on and my husband was standing over me. The tub was no longer filled with water. My clothes were dry. So was the floor. I sat up, alarmed.

"What happened to the water? The floor was all wet...."

"What water? Jesus, Morgan. How much Xanax did you take? Did you wash it down with Chardonnay?" I shook my head as I hauled myself out of the tub. He continued talking, but I didn't hear him. Nothing was registering. There was a slight ringing in my ears, along with something else. A faint sound. A rattle?

"...the call to the insurance company didn't happen, did it? Did you at least manage to call Jenny's orthodontist? Or Paul's teacher to talk about his grade?" He was glaring at me in the mirror while he scrubbed his hands, which our therapist had taught him to do as a calming mechanism. It didn't seem to be working just then.

I shook my head and rubbed my neck. My head was throbbing. "I did manage to lose consciousness three times today." He turned around and rolled his eyes at me before throwing a hand towel into the hamper.

"Great. I guess I'll take care of everything tomorrow between my full day of meetings, plus I have to call your psychiatrist because you clearly need your meds adjusted."

All I could do was stare at the floor in disbelief. I crouched down and touched it while my husband towered over me. *What happened to the water?* I touched my eye and cheek. They felt normal with no sign of injury. My husband scoffed under his breath and left me squatting there.

"Can you drag a comb through your hair? The kids will be home soon and they need dinner before going out with their friends tonight," he shouted over his shoulder as he left the room.

I stood up and examined my reflection. There were no bruises on my face. I took my hair out of its bun and brushed it furiously, tugging too hard on my roots so that I could make sure that they, at least, were real. I brushed and brushed until my eyes watered. My nervous system appeared to be fully intact, and the Xanax had finally kicked in. Whatever I had seen or experienced, it wasn't the Xanax. Those side effects had become second nature to me: drowsiness, turning the brain into a bit of a sludge, trouble accessing just the right word. That had not been my experience. At all.

I walked into the kitchen. The lights fried my eyes, and I couldn't stop myself from thinking that my glistening counters looked like an autopsy table. I pulled some fresh, organic chicken breasts from the fridge and sliced into them the way a coroner would. The whole kitchen instantly smelled of raw flesh. My husband had gone downstairs to the family room, where he would spend the rest of the night staring at his phone, as the kids came bolting through the door, already arguing.

"MOM! Tell Paul not to tell James Maxwell that I have a crush on him!"

"Mom! Tell Jenny to please keep her mouth closed because her brace face is terrifying!"

"Well, at least I'll have nice teeth, not like your gross yellow ones!"

"I'm gonna tell James you still wet the bed!"

"MOM!"

"Knock it off!" My husband's voice bellowed from downstairs, which would be the extent of his parenting for the evening.

I placed a perfunctory plateful of balance between protein and vegetables in front of my family, which finally lured my husband out of his lair. Everyone ate, complained about my cooking, stared at their phones, and left their dishes on the counter for me to clean. I looked around during dinner, but there was no sign of the ghost anywhere. She was gone. *Thank goodness.* But that initial feeling of relief was replaced almost immediately by other, more complicated ones that I couldn't put my finger on. Could I actually have *missed* having her around? In spite of her vengeful and apparently murderous tendencies, she had sparked the most life and excitement that I had felt for a long time. And, after all, she hadn't actually harmed me....

After dinner, everyone ran out the door—my husband included.

"Where are you going?"

"I told you. I am meeting a client for a drink."

Yeah, right. "That's right. Good luck!" I forced a cheery tone into my voice and smiled. He gave me a friendly kiss on the cheek before leaving.

I cleaned up dinner, poured a glass of wine, and walked into the bathroom. Once again, I stared at my reflection in the mirror over our matching his-and-hers sinks. I could feel my 17-year-old self-curling up deep inside of me to once again go dormant, leaving me alone in my middle-aged body. Somehow the tense tonic of my family relationships had simultaneously spooked her and drained her of hope. I felt crumpled and it showed in my face.

"It's ok. They're gone. You can come back," I told the ghost and took a huge swig of wine. For a brief moment, I felt a pang of disappointment that she might not return.

I heard the rattle before I saw her again in the mirror behind me—bloodshot eye and all—and lifted my wine glass in a cheers gesture before draining it. And then, I did something I had prevented myself from doing for years: I cried. I leaned against the counter, rested my head on my arms, and released big, heaving sobs. I cried because I was more afraid of what my life had become than I was of this ghost. I cried because my relationships were fractured like a pane of paper-thin glass. I cried because my dreams were ghosts themselves. And I cried because sometimes fighting—and surviving—against my own mental illness left me too depleted to go on.

She would've gone away if I had finished the ritual. I knew that. But I didn't want to make her go away. I knew when I turned around that the bathtub would be full again. Somehow, she had heard me. Somehow, she understood what it was I actually needed.

I took off my clothes and, for once, didn't bother to put them in the hamper. She had drawn my bath and the water was steaming slightly, just like I liked it. I walked to it solemnly, with a degree of ceremony and respect that all rites of passage deserved. First, I submerged one foot, then another, and then my imperfect body. And then my beautiful face and hair. When I was fully underwater, I opened my eyes.

She was standing next to the tub, and through the water, her skin looked translucent, showing the bones and veins below. Her lips began to dissolve, leaving behind a ghoulish grin. Then, the skin over her cheekbones, nose, forehead, and chin began to dissolve. Her wet tangle of black hair fell to the floor, leaving behind only a skull. It was white and pristine.

As it turns out, you can hear a death rattle more clearly underwater. Ours clamored together for a moment in a ghastly harmony. And then, we were both free.

The Hide-and-Seek Game

I should have known better than to play with a doll as an adult. But then, that was the whole problem: I didn't feel much like an adult. I had been out of college for three years already and didn't have much to show for it. I had moved to L.A. to become a rock star and instead ended up in a band whose best gig is performing at a roller-skating rink in the San Fernando Valley twice a month. My day job had evolved from barista to vintage store clerk to spa booking coordinator, so at least my salary was growing little by little. Still, it was nothing to submit to the Class Notes section of my college magazine—the place reserved for success stories, wedding photos, and baby announcements.

When I took my yearly summer flight from L.A. to Minneapolis, the view out of the plane window was the landscape that had been the backdrop to my formative years, and I could almost see it shrug in disappointment as it prepared for my arrival. There were no tales of being discovered in a tiny local watering hole and being thrust onto a spotlit stage due to the brilliance of my own songwriting. I had achieved no sleek veneer of fame that I could wear around my hometown like a badge of honor, clearly setting me apart from my humble peers.

I had the same ritual at the airport: I would look for Momsy in the baggage claim area and hide from her. Each time, before she saw me, there was always a particular look in her eyes. It was a combination of hope and excitement—a kind of optimism that had no basis in reality. She would be scanning the crowd of strangers, looking for me, hoping that I would be different this time. When she would see me—blue hair, 20-eye black boots, and a frilly white vintage skirt—the look evaporated and her face fell. She would give me a double cheek kiss and a quick scolding for smelling like cigarettes before we picked up my suitcase and guitar from the baggage carousel and headed west to the suburbs.

The more time we spent driving, the bigger the houses got, and the fewer and farther between they were. The concrete palate of highways and a cityscape gave way to thick layers of green whizzing past the car windows. My mom and I had made small talk, mainly in the form of me curtly answering her pointed questions, and then she signaled that our brief period of what passed as bonding was over by turning up the volume on NPR.

"Play it again, Sam!" It was my sister Max's standard greeting when she opened the door before enveloping me in a surprisingly tight bear hug with her bony arms. There we were, polar opposites, impossibly constructed of the same DNA, occupying our shared affectionate space. "I've missed you, Sam! How's your music? You must play something for us before we leave." My sister had somehow managed to grab my guitar, navigate a landmine of plastic doll shoes, pour me a glass of water, and let the dog out in the time it took for me to untie and remove my boots (to be fair, 20 eyes worth of laces takes some finessing). Before I had a chance to answer her question, her oldest daughter—my six-year-old niece, Cleo—had wrapped herself around my waist and legs like a koala bear.

"Fan!" When Cleo was learning to talk, Fan was as close as she could get to Sam, and the name stuck. Two seconds later, my youngest niece, Frances, toddled into the kitchen, wearing nothing but a diaper and her mop of messy blonde hair. She always had the same reaction whenever she saw me: a mass of giggles escaped her mouth like champagne bubbles.

My sister had the house in the suburbs, the cherubic children, the black lab, and the husband in finance. She had neatly slipped into the construct of the life that my parents had intended for both of us—the construct that I had pretty much demolished. She was the Golden Child, the Magnum Opus, the One They Got Right. And she was my favorite person. She sent me encouraging care packages and listened to audio files of my music. She believed in me.

I had come to town to house-and-dog sit while she and my brother-in-law took my nieces up north for a weekend at a friend's cabin. She simply didn't trust anyone else, and Momsy and Papa couldn't be bothered. In exchange for my caretaking, they left me a fully stocked fridge and a fancy computer with oodles of editing tools for music. Plus, I could play my guitar without bothering my roommate, who seemed to sleep for 14 hours a day, or my downstairs neighbor, who jabbed the ceiling with a broom handle at the first pluck of a string.

Momsy, my sister, my brother-in-law, and the nieces all gathered in the living room—at my sister's command—and listened to my latest original song. My nieces bopped around the room while my mother thumbed through a magazine and yawned.

"Sam, you are so talented! Your big break is coming. I can feel it!" My sister clapped and glared at everyone around the room until they joined in.

"Thanks, Max. We shall see!"

The next hour was a blur of zipping up suitcases, wrangling a toddler into clothing, dodging my brother-in-law's pre-travel cursing tirades, and reviewing an extensive list of instructions and chores for each day. Momsy reminded me that she was just down the road if I needed anything—unless of course she was riding her horse or working in her garden or playing bridge, in which case, call someone else. There was a flurry of hugs, kisses, niece nuzzles, last-minute reminders, and, finally, the sound of a garage door closing. Silence. At last.

There is truth to the adage that time flies when you are having fun. In their comfortably finished basement, I became so immersed in my music—the creating of it, the filing down and polishing up and perfecting of it—that before I knew it several hours had passed. Only the steady rumbling of my stomach informed me that it was dinnertime. Rufus, the black lab, had been curled at my feet the whole time, and I figured it was time for both of us to eat.

We climbed the stairs and emerged from the basement. I plopped a cup of dog food into Rufus's bowl and poured the creamy tomato soup my sister always left for me into a pot on the stove. As the dog chomped and the soup warmed, I started scrolling through Instagram. My fellow musician friends seemed to have gigs galore while I was here hanging out with a black lab. I was starting to feel agitated when an incoming call popped up on my screen. It was my friend—sometimes with benefits—who also happened to be named Sam.

"Hey." That was his standard greeting. It was good to hear his voice.

"Hey, yourself! What's up?" I replied.

"I just got back from Japan and thought I'd give you a call and let you know that you don't have to pine for me anymore." Clearly jet lag hadn't impacted his ability to be sarcastic.

"Oh, good," I replied. "I haven't gotten out of bed for a week. I just held your picture and cried."

"I thought as much."

"Ha. So, how was it?"

Sam and I had hooked up during the final week of college, and things between us had been in a weird gray area ever since. He lived in Maine on what was essentially an artist commune, and though he hated cities, he still visited me several times a year. We didn't want to be in a relationship, but we still talked every day. He took fancy trips with his wealthy family several times a year, and he always sent me postcards, which he signed, "Your Whatever." He was not conventionally attractive: he was short and scrawny with angled features and curly hair, and he suffered from debilitating self-consciousness. But our chemistry was otherworldly.

After he told me the main details of his trip—the food, the sights, the obscure Anime that he loved—his responses seemed clipped and almost impatient. It wasn't until we got through the perfunctory details a few minutes later that I realized he had a juicy bit of conversation that he had been wanting to share with me.

"I came across a game you would like."

"Yeah?" I was picturing his lips and only half-listening.

"You would like it because it's terrifying." A shared love of horror movies—especially the older ones with stripped-down special effects and plenty of tense moments—was another thing we had in common.

Apparently, he had spent most of his trip with a "porcelain-skinned, Japanese goth girl with sexy tattoos"—details I did not need—and she had tried to convince him to play the terrifying game. He refused.

"Huh. Interesting. So, tell me about the game." I shrugged off the mention of the girl. After all, he wasn't my boyfriend. He could do whatever he wanted. We both could. I had no reason to be jealous. EXCEPT I WAS.

The girl's name was Aoi and she had taught Sam all about Hitori Kakurenbo: Hide and Seek By Yourself. Except you weren't really by yourself. You were with a doll.

"So, here's what you do, according to Aoi: You cut open the doll, remove its stuffing, and replace it with rice. I guess rice attracts spirits? Then you have to cut your fingernails and put them inside the

196

doll."

"Ew. Why?" I examined my own nails, which were utterly unimpressive with their overgrown cuticles and chipped navy-blue polish.

"Supposedly it connects the doll to your energy." He lowered his voice into a caricature of a spooky whisper. "You know…so that it knows the right person to terrify and possibly kill." He chuckled and brought his voice back to its normal pitch. "Did I mention that I didn't play this game? And that no one should ever?"

"And yet, you felt compelled to share it with me."

"Well, yes, because I knew you'd think it was creepy and cool. But don't get any ideas, Sam…"

"I won't. Don't worry."

Sheesh. He was already such an overly cautious old man. Half the time he wore cardigans with deep pockets that looked like natural dispensers for hard butterscotch candies, like the kind my grandpa used to give me. After assuring him I wouldn't play the game, he gave me the rest of the instructions (or at least what he could remember between sessions of "deep, meaningful, spiritual conversations" with Aoi—gross). First, sew up the doll's rice-and-fingernail-filled innards with red thread, and then wrap the thread around the doll's body a few times before tying it off ("This represents human blood and the circulatory system"). Fill a bathtub with water, and then find a hiding place, place a cup of saltwater in it, and give the creepy doll that is going to kill you later (allegedly) a name. At 3am, head to the bathroom with the doll, and say three times:

"You are the first It!" Then, you place the doll in the bathtub, grab a knife, and turn off the lights. Leave the TV switched to a station showing nothing but static, go to your hiding place, close your eyes, and count to ten.

"At that point, the game is afoot."

"*Afoot*? Who says that?"

"You love it."

"Ha." I DID. "So, what happens next?"

"Well, if you want to end the game, I guess you put some salt water in your mouth, spit it on the doll, and pour the rest over it. Then you yell, 'I win!' three times. But the thing is…"

"Yeah?" I was nervously chipping away at my nail polish.

"The doll won't be in the bathroom where you left it. It'll be…moving around, trying to find you."

An explosion of chills moved along my spine. That fun feeling of fear and excitement—the one that kept me addicted to horror movies—emerged. "That's awesome!"

"No, it's not. It's messed up and scary. Even I won't play around with that stuff. Besides you know that I am scared of two things: spiders and dolls."

We decided to change the subject because I could tell he didn't want to talk about dolls anymore. He told me more about the forest where people go to commit suicide and the hedgehog café where you can play with the prickly little creatures while drinking fancy tea. Japan seemed equal parts dark and adorable, and I couldn't wait to visit one day.

The jet lag was getting to Sam, so we said

goodnight. After playing a quick game of nighttime fetch with Rufus in the well-lit backyard, the two of us retreated once again to the basement to watch some adult cartoons. I figured I deserved a post-dinner whiskey as well.

I changed into the fuzzy PJs my sister had left me, poured myself a drink, and settled in. When Rufus started snoring around 1 a.m., I started feeling restless. I hated this time of night. It was too early for my mind to turn off and go to sleep, but it was too late to do any more creative work.

Around 1:30 a.m. I heard a scratching sound. Mice. Just off of the main part of my sister's basement was an unfinished part that served as a haphazard storage unit, and it held any manner of things, from our old stuffed animals to my niece's onesies that she had outgrown several months earlier. I stood up and stomped on the ground in an attempt to scare the rodents away, but they were not much intimidated by socks on a thick carpet.

I opened the door to the unfinished part of the basement and flipped on the light. The scratching stopped. I glanced around, but nothing was moving. It was always an interesting stroll down memory lane to revisit the objects that were stored there, and I chuckled a little at my sister's cluttered sense of sentimentality.

A little pink lump on top of one pile caught my attention. It was a doll. Specifically, it was a doll that I had bought for Cleo. She had picked it out herself, and I had reluctantly purchased it for her, even though there was something about the toy that didn't seem quite right. The eyes—the kind that opened and shut depending on if the doll was lying down or upright—were just a little too realistic. It had overly rosy cheeks, almost as if it had a fever, and it wore a frilly pink dress dotted with rosebuds. Its golden hair had originally been tied in pigtails with pale blue ribbons, but after my Cleo's experiments with scissors, it was short and uneven with bald spots making her look completely unhinged. My niece lost interest in the doll after that, and I couldn't say I blamed her. As I felt the doll's soft cloth body in my hands, a terrible idea bubbled up.

I have a strange relationship with my own ideas, as many creative types seem to. Sometimes they are nourishing and fortify my existence, like building muscle on a skeletal frame. Other times they are destructive—generated by my brain for the purpose of failing, reinforcing the idea that I will never be good enough, or plotting a dangerous escape from reality. For instance, taking that extra shot of whiskey is never a good idea. In any case, one particular kind of idea entered my head at that moment.

I turned off the light in the basement room and closed the door behind me. I had turned the doll away from me so that I didn't have to look into those glazed-yet-lifelike eyes. I carried it upstairs, put it in a seated position on the kitchen counter, and opened my laptop. Rufus had started whimpering at my feet—a telltale sign that he needed to pee—so I let him outside.

"Let's see. 'Hide and seek with a doll,'" I googled. "Well. If it's good enough for *Aoi*, it's good enough for me." After a few minutes of reading, I felt the doll staring at me so I turned it around to face the other way. Sam had left out some of the more terrifying details in his description. The game was definitely teetering near the precipice of things only totally crazy people do. I could shamelessly admit to myself that I was considering doing it for two reasons: one, to show Sam I was cooler and more fearless than any other girl he knew. And two, hopefully I would be able to write a song or two about the experience.

But as I did my research, I found myself balking a little at this idea. The whole ritual was pretty dark. I picked up the doll, tried in vain to smooth down her Bedhead from Hell, and sighed. A terrible flaw of mine was that once I decided to do something, it was hard to talk myself out of it. Changing my mind makes me feel itchy and agitated, and it was perhaps due to this very flaw that my life was careening on this particularly disappointing-to-parents path. I had been described as "impulsive and stubborn" by my preschool teachers, and not much had changed since then. Unfortunately, I had decided that I wanted to play this weird, dark game, and so I would.

"Wanna play a game?" I said to the doll while I patted its head, making its eyes jiggle a little. I dug through some drawers and cabinets until I found all of the supplies I needed: red thread, a needle, a sharp knife, rice, salt, and fingernail clippers. It felt more like I was preparing a pork roast than a murderous doll. Just off the kitchen was a cozy guest room with its own full bathroom—and, as luck would have it, a deep bathtub. This would be the perfect place to start the ritual. After all, what's the worst thing that could happen in a bathroom that was wallpapered with pictures of green topiaries? I undressed the doll and laid it on the counter. "This won't hurt a bit." I covered its eyes with my hand for good measure and sliced its torso open with the knife. I pulled out its innards and replaced them with rice and my fingernail clippings. Then, using my pathetic sewing skills, I stitched it closed with red thread. The doll looked terrible, so I decided to put its dress back on before wrapping the red thread around it, making sure its arms and legs could still move. I turned the doll over a few times in my hands. If it was really going to come to life, perhaps it would be a good idea to identify its weak spots in the event that I needed to exploit them for my own protection. The biggest weak spot appeared to be its eyelids since they could open and close. "If I run into any trouble, I'll just knock you onto your back," I said to the doll. "If your eyes are closed, you can't see me." I filled the bathtub with water and left the doll on the bathroom counter while I went to set up my hiding place.

The master bedroom and the bedroom my nieces shared were on the opposite end of the house from the kitchen and guest room. Stretching between each end of the house was a long, narrow hallway, which gave the house the shape of a sideways capital I. The equally long and narrow living room shared a wall with the hallway, and one could enter the living room through the kitchen, or through a doorway that was kitty-corner to the master bedroom. The back wall of the living room was made entirely of multiple sliding glass doors that led to a huge backyard. The doors would provide an effective means of escape if needed. The master bedroom had a roomy walk-in closet that I could duck into if necessary, as well as its own door to the backyard. I decided that the master bedroom would be the perfect hiding place.

I mixed a glass of salt water and put it on my sister's nightstand. Then, I heard a noise behind me. It was faint at first, but then it grew louder. A scratching sound. I turned around slowly. The scratching continued. This time, I knew it wasn't mice. Something was scratching against the door that led to the backyard. Then I heard a whimper.

Rufus. I had completely forgotten about him. I opened the door and he nearly knocked me over in a whirl of tail wagging and happy-to-see-you panting. "Sorry, buddy." I patted his big belly and scratched his ears. I was happy that I would have a protector during this game. I had taken care of him when he was a puppy while my sister and brother-in-law were on their honeymoon, and that experience seemed to cement his loyalty to me—even if I tended to forget him outside sometimes.

It was 2:30 a.m. I had 30 minutes until the ritual's mandatory start time of 3:00 a.m. As per the instructions, I turned on the TV in the master bedroom, let Rufus hop into the bed next to me (which was usually a no-no because of the white sheets, but it was Auntie Fan's weekend), and told myself not to succumb to the world's most comfortable mattress. The ritual called for the TV to be turned to a static station, but clearly, the game had been invented before the era of smart TVs, and static was now extinct. I figured I should turn the TV on anyway, even if it didn't have any static, and settled on Cartoon Network's Adult Swim because a little levity felt needed at that moment.

At 3:00 a.m. I told Rufus to stay put, walked across the house to the guest bathroom, and started the ritual. I half expected the doll to be crawling across the ceiling, but it was right where I left it, looking at me with those freakishly sentient eyes. I picked it up.

"Well, I guess I'm supposed to name you. My niece named you Fan, after me, but that just seems too weird..." I eyed the rosebuds on her dress. "I'll call you Rose. Also, try not to be too scary. I'm just trying to impress a guy." I took a deep breath and summoned my most official-sounding voice: "Sam is the first It! Sam is the first It! Sam is the first It!" I placed Rose in the bathtub, picked up the knife, and headed back to the master bedroom. I was supposed to turn all the lights off in the house, but no way was I going to do that. I had no night vision, and I didn't want to have to explain a broken leg due to tripping over a piece of furniture. I sat on the bed next to Rufus and stroked him while I counted to ten, and then walked across the house again to the guest bathroom. Once again, the doll was right where I left her, floating in the tub with her eyes closed.

"I have found you, Rose!" I said with a bit too much enthusiasm before plunging the knife into her rice-filled midsection. "Now Rose is It! Now Rose is It! Now Rose is It!" I backed away slowly, expecting her to do something. Instead, her plastic eyelids stayed closed. "Uh, I'm gonna go hide now. Sorry I stabbed you." I ran back to the master bedroom and joined Rufus on the bed. *Aqua Teen Hunger Force* was on. Perfect. I waited for something to happen, but nothing did. With the steady breathing of the dog next to me, the feeling of the soft mattress underneath me, and the dulcet tones of Master Shake in my ear, I couldn't help but fall asleep.

I woke up to a strange sound. I heard the noises before I opened my eyes and saw the source: the channels were flipping frantically on their own. I shooed Rufus off the bed and felt around in the bedding, convinced that one of us was sitting on the remote. But then I saw it on the nightstand, right where I had left it. I crept toward the TV slowly, and Rufus had taken his hunting dog posture with his eyes alert and ears slightly raised. The same garbled sounds were coming out of the TV over and over again, as the channels would pause just long enough for one word to be uttered. It wasn't until I put my ear close to the speaker that my brain could wrap itself around what the voices were saying:

"Where. Are. You?"

I turned off the TV and looked at Rufus. He looked alarmed and cocked his head a little. This had to be some kind of electrical malfunction, and my mind was simply piecing together speech patterns that weren't actually there. I remembered from my Psych class freshman year that the brain will strain to make patterns, even when there are none. This was clearly the explanation. I needed to stay calm and keep my wits about me. "It's only a doll," I told Rufus.

I opened the door to the hallway. It was empty, and the house was silent. At least for a moment. The sound was hard to make out at first. Tap, tap, tap, tap. Pause. Tap, tap, tap, tap. Pause. It was getting closer.

I ran a mental inventory of all the things it could be. The house settling. Branches hitting the outside walls. Erratic rainfall. But I knew it was none of those things. Slowly, I walked from the doorway of the master bedroom through the arch of the doorway into the living room, scanning the floor with my eyes as the realization of what was happening landed in my bones like lead, even before I saw her. Standing next to an armchair, staring at me, was Rose.

"Holy—"

Rufus let out a single bark from the safety of the master bedroom, and as if by his command I retreated back into it and shut the door, diving under the covers. Rufus jumped onto the bed and laid his body on top of mine, protecting me. We were both listening. On the other side of the bedroom wall, the tapping continued. Tap, tap, tap, tap, pause. Tap, tap, tap, tap, pause. She was making her way through the living room. A low growl started in Rufus's belly. It moved through his throat and resonated in his mouth before he let out a jarring bark and scrambled off the bed. He began scratching at the bedroom door and sniffing underneath it, whimpering and growling and barking.

"Rufus! Stop it!" He became more and more worked up in spite of my commands to bring him back to bed. He began clawing at the door, and I was so worried that he would destroy it—and I would have to face my sister's wrath—that I finally gave him what he wanted. I opened the door, and like a shameless coward, immediately shut it behind him. Even through the closed door, I could hear everything: Rufus running into the living room, growling and barking. Scuffling. Teeth snapping. Doll footsteps tapping. Yelping—a painful, screeching exclamation of pain. I put my hand on the doorknob, readying myself to rescue him when I heard a sickening crunch. Rufus let out a squeal. And then, silence.

An eternity passed. Longer. My fear drained and was replaced with concern for Rufus. My fur nephew. No matter what was waiting for me, I needed to get to him. I took a fortifying breath, opened the door, and strode determinedly into the living room. Rufus was a dark, motionless heap in the far corner. I couldn't tell if he was breathing. His head looked like it was at an unnatural angle. Standing next to him with her back to me was Rose.

"Rufus!" I clasped both hands over my mouth. I hadn't meant to make any noise. The pathetic semblance of a plan I had made was to sneak up on the doll, catch her, douse her in saltwater, and end the ritual. But that plan was shot.

Slowly, the doll's head began to turn. And turn. And turn. Her head was on backward, and she was staring at me.

I took my hands down and opened my mouth, but no scream emerged. My vocal cords were paralyzed, but luckily my feet weren't. I ran back to the master bedroom, grabbed the glass of salt water, and picked up the knife. By the time I made it back to the living room, the doll was nowhere to be seen. Not good.

I looked at the lump in the corner that was Rufus. There was nothing I could do for him at the moment. I knew he was dead, and I wasn't prepared to face it. I needed to find this doll and end the ritual before anything else terrible happened. I stood still, listening. The TV in the living room turned on and the volume blared, causing me to jump. I whirled around and found myself holding the knife in a defensive stance as if it was a sword. The channels flipped erratically, just as they had in the bedroom.

"Where. Are. You? Where. Are. You?" I ran to the wall and unplugged it. Silence. And then, tap, tap, tap, tap, pause. She was in the kitchen. I tiptoed into the hallway, cringing as the floorboards groaned beneath me. I had never noticed that Max's floors made so much noise. First, I took a step. Creak. Then the doll responded by taking her own steps. Tap. The walk down the hallway to the kitchen was long and laborious, but I finally got there. Carefully, I peered in. She was nowhere to be seen. I crouched, readying the saltwater. *Come out, come out, wherever you are, you little b—*

My thought was interrupted when I saw her, half-hidden, behind the kitchen island. She was peeking around the corner at me and seemed so childlike, playing with me. But her face was menacing, and the air turned ice cold. It took a moment for the shock to wear off for me to register that she was walking toward me, remarkably quickly and easily, and before I knew it she was right in front of me. I forgot the tools in my hands, and all I could think to do was kick her over as I jumped back, spilling saltwater on myself and letting out an involuntary shriek. She was on her back with her eyes closed and once again seemed like a lifeless doll. Thank goodness. I had been right about her movable eyelids being her weak spot after all. I took a breath and felt my body relax before emptying what was left of the saltwater into my mouth, preparing to spit it on her.

I stood over her. And then her arms moved. I watched as she brought her hands to her face, and her tiny fingers touched the ends of her eyelashes. *No,* I thought to myself. *You are not supposed to be moving. Your eyes are closed.* With a delicate popping sound, she removed her eyelids and the glassy, horrifying roundness of her eyes had more life in them than they did before. In my state of shock, I did the one thing you are not supposed to do in this game: I swallowed the saltwater. I also peed my pants, but there was no rule against that.

In an instant, she was on her feet, and I was on the ground, having tripped over one of Rufus's chew toys, but also, because my feet didn't remember how they worked. The glass shattered as I fell and the knife slid across the floor. She was unbelievably fast, and with those crazed eyes and hair, she ran right past me. I was paralyzed as she bent stiffly from her waist and picked up the knife.

Then, almost as if she was on a rotating pedestal, she turned in one smooth movement and faced me. I had inadvertently given a doll that I had brought to life a knife. Not good.

I was only a few feet from the guest room and crawled quickly to it on my hands and knees, but she was right behind me. I felt a searing pain in my leg just before reaching the door, which I somehow managed to kick shut behind me. I clicked the lock and pulled a chair under the doorknob before inspecting my leg. The doll had stabbed me in the left calf, leaving a gushing wound several inches deep. I felt briefly dizzy and told myself not to look at it too closely.

"You BITCH!" I yelled to the door. I hobbled to the bathroom and grabbed one of my sister's charming antique tea towels from the rack to stop the bleeding. I knew she was going to kill me for that. Luckily, being a parent to young children—and a tad on the overly cautious side—had taught my sister to stock all of the bathrooms in the house with first aid materials. They were mostly petite band-aids decorated with princesses, but they were better than nothing. After using an entire box, I knew that the bleeding would hold for a little while.

I was so distracted by my flesh wound that the sound coming from the bedroom door didn't register right away. It was so light and steady at first that it could have been a ticking clock. But then it became louder and more erratic. I left the bathroom and stood near the bedroom door, watching it jolt in its hinges. She was stabbing the door with the knife.

I was cornered in this bedroom, and one way or

another a murderous doll was going to find a way in eventually. I sat on the bed and did something I hadn't done in years: burst into tears. I was so scared, and so alone, and had caused the death of the World's Best Dog. There was no one who could help me. As I sobbed, I realized that the feelings of aloneness had lived in my gut for the last few years, dormant, waiting for a moment like this. Once I felt them there, they took over my entire body, and I convulsed in my sadness and hurt and anger. Still, she stabbed the door, and the sound of wood splintering against metal began to rival my tears in its volume level. But then, just as quickly as it began, my storm passed. The tears and snot stopped. My body relaxed. The critical voices that had spun in my head like whirling dervishes were still. The stabbing continued. And I decided I had had just about enough.

Forget Sam and his complicated feelings. Forget Momsy and the plastic surgery-altered nose of hers that was perfect for looking down at me. Forget the crappy band that was holding me back. Forget my inner critic. And forget. This. Doll.

I found the bath salts that were perched on the edge of the tub and dumped out the marble toothbrush holder that was by the sink. I made what I knew would be a disgusting saltwater mixture and put my hand on the doorknob. Deep breath. I could do this.

I opened the door, and within a split second I was once again flat on my back, and the cup of saltwater was splashed across the floor. Somehow the doll had knocked me off my feet. She was standing on my stomach with both hands raised over her head, holding the knife. I grabbed her around the waist to try and throw her off, but I couldn't move her. It was as if she suddenly weighed a ton, even though where she stood on my body felt like I was bearing a normal doll weight. I tried to wrestle her off of me and gave it everything I had. But she was too strong. Her unblinking eyes met mine and I took a breath and held it. I knew in a moment that knife would be plunged into my chest and that would be it.

I closed my eyes. My ears were filled with a clattering sound and then a loud chomp. I opened my eyes, and the doll was on her back next to me. A dark, hulking shape stood over her. Rufus! I found the toothbrush holder, which still had some salt water in it, poured it into my mouth, and spit it out over the doll. "I win! I win! I win!" I shouted before grabbing the knife from her hand, cutting the red thread that was still tied around her dress, and, as per the ritual instructions, stabbing her repeatedly until the rice spilled from her body and all over the floor like white gore. I waited, half-expecting her to move, but she lay still. It was over. Still, just in case, I put the knife on a table and out of her reach.

I examined Rufus while he whimpered in pain. One of his hind legs hung loosely behind him and he was bleeding from his mouth. I looked at my calf. The blood had begun to seep through the band-aids. We both needed medical attention.

I called Momsy. "I need you to come right away."

"It's 6 A.M.!!"

"No questions. I need you. Now. Get over here."

While I waited for her, I coaxed Rufus to his dog bed in the mudroom, wrapped the doll in an old rag, and brought it out to the garage. Everything I needed was right there: an empty garbage can, a can of gasoline, and a box of matches for lighting backyard bonfires. I pushed a button and the garage door growled open. I pulled everything onto the driveway and tossed the doll into the garbage can before dousing it in gasoline, lighting a match, and dropping it in. A plasticky smell rose into the air and the smoke was pitch black. Later, when it was done burning, I would bury the ashes deep in the forest.

Momsy came roaring up the driveway in her SUV, with as much concern on her face as she could manage with the Botox. She didn't ask questions—at least not just yet. Together, we wrapped Rufus in a blanket and carried him, carefully, to the car.

"I didn't do this. This wasn't my fault. Something...bad happened."

"You have got some serious explaining to do."

I waited to tell her everything until after we had taken Rufus to the vet. He had a broken hip, which would require surgery and a cast, some bruised ribs, and a tender abdomen, which required time and rest. But he would be fine.

As we drove back to my sister's house, I told Momsy everything. There was really no sugar coating or stretching of the truth that would make the story any more palatable, and so I just went full

213

steam ahead and disclosed it all. I fully expected a shocked lecture, or an immediate appointment booking with a psychiatrist, or banishment from my family kingdom. After asking some bewildered clarifying questions, she nodded and reached over to pat my knee. We drove along in silence for a few more minutes. I felt as though I was receiving understanding and even sympathy from her for one of the first times ever. I held my breath, hoping that this was where she would leave it.

"Well, I certainly don't fault you a, well, *youthful indiscretion.* I trust you will make better decisions in the future. There will be hell to pay with your sister, and so you do not need to hear my thoughts on the matter as well."

Classic Momsy uppercut. The disdain and disapproval was palpable in that car, even if I couldn't read it on her glazed and spackled face. But, for once, I didn't actually care.

She was right, though: there was hell to pay with my sister when I called her on the phone that evening. Rufus was essentially her third child. She had also hissed through clenched teeth that she knew something was off about that doll. Upon returning from her trip, she burned all of the dolls that the girls no longer played with, and that seemed to have any hint of life in their glassy eyes. Eventually, Rufus healed and so did my relationship with my sister. I just had to pledge that there would be no future shenanigans of any kind in her home.

My leg had required stitches. But I was more than fine. After that night, something in me had crossed over, and I was never going back. Things were going to be different for me. I had won against a murderous doll. There was no limit to what I could do. The earth itself could quake and gape beneath my feet, but I would stay put, buoyed by my own artistic-if-somewhat-angsty variety of personal magma. Nothing would make me crumble. Not even the supernatural.

The Ouija Board

Unlike the rest of the stories in this collection, this one is a true firsthand account of my own experience playing a ghost game. One night while at my friend Kate's (her name has been changed) house, we decided to play with a Ouija Board. Ouija Boards are certainly not to be trifled with, as innocuous as they may seem, and it was a lesson we both learned that night. These events happened in the late 90s when we were juniors in high school, and neither one of us has played with a Ouija Board since. Like all of the games in this book, if you choose to play with a Ouija Board, you play at your own risk.

A little context: Kate's house was located on a quiet street in an even quieter Minneapolis, Minnesota suburb. It was the last house you would expect to be haunted, and yet it was. It was also the last place you might expect some terrible evil force to be unleashed, and yet, it appears as though we managed that as well. We made the choice to play with the Ouija Board in an attempt to communicate with the entities in her house. We were also extremely bored and filled with nearly fatal amounts of ennui. We were teenagers, after all.

One helpful piece of information to note: back in the 90s there were no streaming services and DVDs had not been popularized yet. We used VCRs to watch movies on videotapes that had actual tape in them, and which we always had to rewind before returning.

I can assure you that what you are about to read is entirely true.

***

"I ate so much today," I moaned as I curled up into the fetal position on Kate's floor. Kate was in the corner of her room re-organizing her bookshelf and CD collection.

I was in pain. Physical pain from my acidic stomach, yes, but also that particular variety of teenager-specific pain. I had broken up with my first love, I was fighting constantly with my parents, and my grades and friendships were in a state of flux. My weight seemed to be a small corner of my existence that I could control. And every day I would sweep and scrub that corner clean.

"Hmm," Kate had uttered in response from her spot on the bed. She was fully immersed in her task and not really listening. I continued anyway.

"I had a piece of toast, a cup of soup, an apple, a handful of popcorn, and a rice cake. I feel like such a cow."

"Hmm."

We had just survived a particularly brutal Minnesota winter, and that year had brought an unseasonably warm spring. On that day in particular, the temperature spiked high enough that it was necessary to switch on Kate's inefficient ceiling fan. I watched it strain and cast shadows on the ceiling without providing any real change in room temperature.

I listened to my stomach growl, voicing its disagreement with my quantitative measure of "too much" food, and felt sick of myself. I was sick of this internal calculus of food versus body image, I was sick of my faux modesty about how much I had eaten, I was sick of whining, and I was sick of my friend not listening to my whining. I needed something to snap me out of my funk. It had to be just the right thing. I rolled onto my stomach and watched Kate comparing two books, as apparently, she had decided to arrange them according to size this time. Watching movies usually helped, but I didn't feel like watching a comedy. I mean, I wanted to feel better, but not entirely shed my feelings of angst. After all, I had some dark poetry to write later.

Horror movies were always a favorite of Kate's and mine, but somehow that option didn't seem dark or exciting enough. A grin spread across my face. What would be dark and exciting was poking and prodding the resident entities in Kate's house.

I sat up. "Kate?"

"Hmm?"

"Do you have a Ouija Board?"

***

The previous summer I had spoken with my friend's mother, who was a gifted psychic. She warned me that the Ouija Board was the most dangerous thing to come out of a toy store, save for Children's Tylenol-sized batteries.

"Here's the thing," she had said matter-of-factly, peering at me over her bifocals. "That thin little piece of cardboard can act like a doorway for spirits, and through it, they can pass between their world and ours *whenever they please*. And not just any spirits. The Ouija Board appeals to the lowest common denominator of spirits. It's like the McDonald's of the spirit world: just like a health-conscious person wouldn't eat at McDonald's, the spirits on higher planes don't come near Ouija Boards. They are far too evolved for that nonsense."

I looked over at my friend, her daughter, who was plucking out a tune on her guitar. She was used to these conversations between her friends and her mother.

"In other words, these are not the spirits you want in your home," my friend's mother continued. "These spirits are the vermin of the spirit world. And, like vermin, they're impossible to get out of your house once they're there. If there's one, there's one hundred."

I asked her about the seemingly authentic conversation I had with my deceased great-grandmother during a Ouija Board session, and in this conversation ,the planchette spelled out things that only my great-grandmother would know. My friend's mother let out a laugh.

"You think that was really your great-grandmother? Oh, absolutely not. The spirits that come through the Ouija Board inhabit the lower astral planes—think murderers and folks who lived dark, violent lives. The choices they made in life have imprisoned them in their rage and hate. Like I said, vermin." She took a thoughtful sip of the hibiscus tea she had grown and brewed herself. "But they are very good at pretending to be other, benevolent spirits—like your grandmother—as a way of luring you in and gaining your trust. They figure out information about you the same way those scam psychics do: by letting you lead them to the answer without realizing it."

"But what can they really do besides scare you?"

"Sorry to beat a dead horse here, so to speak, but again, you have to think of them as vermin. It's a frustrating experience to have your house overrun by mice. It makes you irritated and stressed, and in some cases, the mice can even make you sick. The same thing happens when your house is infested with spirits, except you can't see them, which makes them even more dangerous. Instead of droppings, they leave behind bad thoughts and feelings. They breed depression and anxiety. Suddenly you don't feel like yourself and you don't quite know why."

"So, how do you get rid of them?"

"It takes someone really in tune with the spirit world to not only get rid of them but to make sure that they stay where they belong. Don't let the Parker Brothers logo fool you: the Ouija Board is not some harmless game."

I shrugged off these warnings the same way I shrugged off the ones from the Surgeon General each time I lit a cigarette. *Oh well. Whatever. I'm sure they're just overreacting. It'll be fine.* And, of course, my go-to line whenever I threw caution to the wind: *Other people might get sick or have bad experiences, but nothing bad is going to happen to ME.*

Kate, of course, not only had a Ouija Board, but she was equally excited about this idea. She unearthed it from its spot between Monopoly and The Ungame, and we knew exactly where we wanted to play it.

Kate's brother's room had been hers when she was younger, before he was born. In both bedrooms, a row of thin rectangular windows lined the back wall near the ceiling, which opened onto a view of a grove of spindly pine trees that were planted next to the house. Before her brother was born, in her original bedroom, Kate's bed had been situated so that she was facing the windows. One night she woke up from a dreamless sleep and noticed two faint glows—one in the corner of the room and one outside the window, almost as if it was suspended in the trees. When her eyes had adjusted fully, she realized that she was looking at two apparitions, both of them men.

"Hi," she said to them. Her reaction was both surprising and also completely representative of Kate as a child. She was almost recklessly bold—a trait that seemed to disintegrate with each year as she got older. In any case, something in her knew to not be afraid of these apparitions, and in fact, she found herself comforted by their presence. Neither apparition spoke, but they both smiled kindly. For a while, they were a part of her nightly routine, like brushing her teeth: she would wake up in the middle of the night, and they would be there. She thought of them as guardian angels and would often speak to them in the darkness of her bedroom. But one night, she awoke and they were gone. Kate waited night after night, but they didn't return. She missed their presence so much that she began to cry—big, heaving sobs that her mom happened to hear during a midnight trip to the kitchen for a glass of water.

"What is it, sweetie?"

"The men are gone."

"What men?"

"There were two men in my room. They come into my room every night. And now they're gone."

When Kate described the men, her mother grew quiet and stern, and Kate thought she had done something wrong. Her mother said nothing as she tucked Kate back into bed, and Kate never saw the men again. It would be several years—long after Kate had switched bedrooms to the one across the hall—before Kate's mother would tell her that they fit the description of her brothers, Kate's uncles. One brother, the ghost in the corner, had died suddenly on his wedding day. The other, the ghost outside, had disappeared without a trace while hiking and was never found.

The ghostly activity, however, didn't stop once Kate moved out of that room. One night, when Kate's brother was two years old, everyone in the house was suddenly awoken by the sound of him screaming. Kate and her parents came running.

They found him standing under the windows— the same windows where Kate had seen her uncle's ghost hovering outside. In his broken toddler

English, he wove together a distraught story: he woke up suddenly, just in time to see an old woman "float sideways" through the rectangular windows.

He struggled to describe her—both his limited vocabulary and hysteria provided an obstacle—but he did manage to say that she was hunched over, wore a white nightgown, had long white hair, and sharp teeth.

She had reached out her wiry arms, picked him up out of bed, and took him to the windows. She had tried to take him out the windows but they didn't fit. She just held him a while, humming, at which point he started screaming. She set him down and floated back through the narrow panes of glass.

Kate's parents had assured her brother that it had all been a bad dream, and his mother stayed in his bedroom, hugging him, singing to him, and putting him back to sleep. Kate's father had escorted Kate back across the hallway and commanded her to go back to sleep. Kate could hear through the walls that it took her brother a long time to stop crying. She could hear the soft murmur of her mother's singing voice. To help herself fall back asleep she pulled the covers over her head, giving herself a warm, dark cocoon.

Her brother never spoke of the woman again. She was simply gone, just like Kate's uncles. But still, the room always gave Kate an unsettled feeling – "the willies," she called it.

Another entity that may have also been haunting Kate's house – the energy did seem rather crowded in there – was the house's previous owner. It was a woman named Helen, who by all accounts had been kindly but quiet and kept mostly to herself. Sadly, she passed away in the house. When Kate was in junior high her mother had purchased an antique mirror, which she hung at the end of the hallway between the two bedrooms in order to make the house seem more spacious. After a few months, the top of the mirror seemed to be slowly wearing away, as if the glass was being rubbed thin, revealing the reflective paper underneath. It happened so subtly and over such a long period of time that no one really seemed to notice it. Finally, one day Kate's mother was walking down the hallway when she saw it: the random patterns of wear weren't so random after all. They spelled out the word "HELEN."

Kate's mother was not one to believe in ghosts, but she was also not one for unnecessarily scaring her children, who seemed to have overactive imaginations already. After that day the mirror was covered with an old bedsheet and banished to the garage.

Kate avoided going into her brother's room as much as possible, but on that particular spring day, I gave her no choice in the matter. The room seemed to be the epicenter of the paranormal activity in the house. It was the perfect place for a Ouija Board session. She balked a little at first and argued that the well-lit kitchen would do the trick just as well, but eventually, she agreed. I could tell that she was feeling that same thrilling combination of fear and excitement as I was.

***

We waited until after the sun had finished setting completely and then we got to work. We lit candles and conducted the first of our "shadow inspections": a thorough examination of the room to make sure that no objects were casting ghostly shadows that could scare or confuse us during the session. After moving some of her brother's He-Man action figures from where they were displayed, and whose shadows were surprisingly daunting, we were ready to start. We sat with our legs crisscrossed, brought our knees together, and balanced the Ouija board on top. Kate placed the planchette in the middle of the board and we touched it gently with our fingertips.

"Let's close our eyes, take a breath, and clear our minds," I said, authoritatively. After my mind felt sufficiently clear, I opened my eyes. "Is there anyone here with us? Does anyone wish to speak to us?"

Like many previous Ouija Board sessions, I had conducted, clearly against the advice of my friend's psychic mother, this one got off to a slow start. After asking several open-ended questions, that flimsy plastic indicator still had not moved. I decided to see if I could get the ball rolling a bit.

"May we speak to the old woman who climbed through the window?"

Slowly, joltingly, the indicator began to move.
Hi.

"Hi," I answered back. I looked up at Kate. She was looking at the planchette intently. I could tell that she wasn't intending to speak just yet, so I continued.

"Do you have a name?"

The planchette moved over a string of letters that spelled out gibberish. It was starting to pick up speed and move with greater fluidity.

"Are you in the room with us?"

YES.

The yes and no parts of the Ouija Board always seemed to be overly emphatic with their bold, capital letters, as if the spirit was screaming the answer.

"Can you prove it?" I felt my stomach lurch a little as I asked this question. I was nervous that something scary might happen, but also almost deliriously hoping that it would. Again, that simultaneous feeling of fear and excitement was almost an addiction for me, and it was the clear driving force in eventually choosing horror as my writing genre of choice.

YES. The planchette moved to the letter W and stayed there. When it did, I turned around to look at the narrow rectangular windows.

W. Window. A feeble voice whispered in my head. She had come through the windows.

I turned back to the board. Kate seemed to be almost catatonic as she stared at the planchette.

I continued. "Let me ask you again: What is your name?"

The answer was gibberish, and the planchette stopped on the letter W. I turned around and looked out the window. Everything looked normal.

Several minutes passed and the planchette stayed still. We asked to speak to Helen, and received no response. We asked to speak to Kate's uncles, and again, nothing. I finally asked to speak to anyone who would be willing to talk to us, and still, we waited. I was about to abandon the session entirely when the plastic under our fingers jolted to life.

IBRINGAVIOLENTFUTURE.

It took Kate and me some time to process what we had just read. There were so many letters strung together so quickly. It spelled the words again, and this time we got it: I BRING A VIOLENT FUTURE.

"Um. Ok. Hi there," I said, nervously. That seemed to be an aggressive statement after such a long period of inactivity.

Kate dislodged her eyes from the planchette and looked at me. We sat there for a moment, letting the message sink in. After some time passed, I spoke again.

"What do you mean by 'a violent future?'" Kate shot me a look and I shrugged. It sounded like a strange thing to ask when I said it out loud, but I was legitimately curious. The indicator began to move again, more rapidly this time.

I BRING YOU PAIN.

Once again, Kate and I looked at each other. I could hear her draw a breath and hold it.

I continued. "Do you....do you want to hurt us?"

YES.

"How do you want to hurt us?"

No response. I asked the question again. The

planchette stayed still.

"So… Can you hurt us?"

NO.

"Why not?"

BECAUSE YOU LIVE.

The planchette moved to the letter W. I turned around and looked at the windows with a distinct feeling of "the willies." This time, for some reason, I was half expecting to see the woman climbing through them. I didn't know for certain if the letter W was even connected to the window at all. I just knew that something about the windows kept drawing my attention to them and compelling me to turn around. Each time I did, nothing was there.

It started to grow hotter in the room, and I could see the sweat beading on Kate's forehead in the candlelight. I wanted to turn on the overhead fan, but I also didn't want to move and break whatever communication was happening with this spirit. Though I didn't want to admit it, I was starting to feel scared, and the heat felt almost like a security blanket. It was best to just stay put and sweat.

"What kind of entity are you?" Kate rolled her eyes at me and I shrugged. It was another strange question, but I had no idea what we were dealing with.

At first, there was nothing, and then a string of gibberish. I decided to be more specific.

"Are you… *a demon*?" I whispered the words. Kate's eyes became wide and she took her fingers off the planchette as if it had become suddenly electrified.

"Why would you ask it that?"

"I mean, I don't know! I have no idea what kind of spirit we are talking to! If we are speaking to a demon, I'd like to at least have that information…"

Kate gave me a stern look, and I wasn't sure she was going to be willing to continue. She eventually shook her head, sighed resignedly, and put her fingers back on the planchette. I could see that her curiosity was getting the better of her.

The second she did it sprang into action. HATE. ANGER. RAGE. The temperature in the room continued to climb and we continued to sweat. The candles flickered and the shadows danced, and Kate and I let a long silence fall.

We heard something coming down the hall, shuffling along the carpet and making the floorboards creak. We both held our breath, listening, and waiting as the sound came closer.

"Sparky!" a moment later her dog, Sparky, entered the room and began sniffing urgently at both of us. I jolted, surprised by his presence, surprised that anything outside of that room actually existed. Kate removed one hand from the planchette to pet him. We both giggled, and it felt good to break the tension for a moment. He looked up at the windows behind me, let out a soft whimper, and bolted from the room.

"Uh…." was the only response I could muster.

Once again, I turned around and looked at the windows. Nothing was there.

I turned back to Kate.

"Yeah. Maybe that's not …so…good…" Kate

said, nodding in the direction of her departed dog.

The air in the room was almost unbearable—hot and thick, making it difficult to breathe. Kate, who had asthma, began to wheeze softly. We both took a brief stretch break and did a quick shadow check. Everything in the room looked normal. We placed our hands back on the planchette.

It began to move again.

I NEED YOU.

We both stared at the board, then at each other.

I NEED YOU, the planchette spelled out again.

I didn't really want to ask the next question, but we had come this far.

"What…do you mean…you need us?"

I WILL TAKE YOU. It moved to the letter W. This time I didn't turn around.

I had to keep going. "Where do you want to take us?" I said in a meek voice.

No response.

"Where do you want to take us?" I repeated, a little louder this time. There was no response, which made me even more nervous.

After what seemed like forever had gone by without a response, my anxiety began to shift into frustration. What kind of spirit makes a vague threat and then doesn't answer follow-up questions? Answer: a rude one. I rolled my eyes and asked the question again, more forcefully this time:

"Where do you want to take us?"

No response.

"Good God, just answer the question!"

GOD ISN'T HERE.

I knew then that things had crossed a line. In

spite of the heat, I felt a shiver. I spoke the words that I had just read out loud and then peeled my eyes from the planchette to look at Kate. I opened my mouth to suggest that we flee the room but stopped short. Kate was looking behind me at the windows, and the color had drained from her already pale face. Her typical expression of terror—a cartoonish popping of her eyes—displayed itself relentlessly.

"Brooke..." she said in a tone that was equally soft and deadly serious. My heart began ramming against my ribs, and I wondered if it was possible to bruise them from the inside. I knew that tone. I hated that tone.

"What?" I whispered. She was frozen in place, her eyes fixed intently on something.

"What?" I said, more loudly this time.

No response.

My anxiety kicked in, and I raised my voice. "FOR THE LOVE OF GOD, WHAT?"

"Move your head," she said, finally.

I couldn't. I was frozen, staring into her face. Her eyes didn't move from whatever it was she was looking at. "No..." I said.

Her voice dropped to a growling whisper. "Move. Your. Head."

I willed my head to move back and forth. When I did, it looked as though she might cry. She raised her index finger and pointed.

"Whose shadow is that?"

It took an eternity, but once again I willed my head to move—this time to look behind me. On the small piece of wall next to the windows—where I had been looking all night—was a black figure. Its head was turned in partial profile. I could see its nose, its neck, and its broad shoulders. Below the shoulders, it tapered off into a narrow, amorphous shape. It was darker than a shadow would have been, and lacked the flickering borders characteristic of one in candlelight.

We sat there for what felt like a long time, forcing our eyes to process what they were seeing. The heat in the room was unbearable, and my skin felt as though it was being swarmed by small electric shocks. The hair on the back of my neck felt as though it would just go ahead and detach itself. I heard a light, high-pitched frequency in both of my ears, and my eyes traced the black outline repeatedly, committing every inch to memory, convincing myself that I was seeing something that wasn't there before. My brain began to feel foggy, devoid of any thoughts. The high-pitched noise began to grow louder and fill my ears entirely.

Kate. I suddenly remembered Kate.

When I turned and looked at her, I could see that she was transfixed. Her head was slightly cocked to the side, the way one is when listening to a story. She even nodded slightly, and one eyebrow was slightly raised. Her trademark "I'm paying attention to you" mannerisms.

Whatever this thing was, it was speaking to her.

"KATE!" I yelled. She blinked, snapping out of it. "WE NEED TO GET THE FUCK OUT OF HERE." I blew out the candles—a shred of common sense kicked in and I knew we didn't need to be starting any fires that night—and Kate followed me out of the bedroom and down the hallway. She scrambled to grab her car keys from the hook by the door; I was already waiting by her car. As she ran out of the house, Sparky started to follow, and we both called out to him, trying to get him to join us in the car. He cocked his head to the side before shrinking backward and disappearing into the house.

"He's never done that before!" Kate said, her face stricken.

"Kate, let's get out of here! Please!"

Kate put her trusty brown Honda into reverse and peeled out of the driveway. As if on autopilot, the car guided us to the one universal sanctuary for all suburban teenagers: a coffee shop.

As we sipped our lattes—the caffeine doing nothing to calm our nerves—everything around us felt surreal. It's alienating being in the same room as a bunch of strangers who can in no way relate to an experience you've just had.

At least I had Kate. She hadn't said a word since placing her coffee order, and I didn't intend to push her. At least the color was starting to return to her face.

"Brooke?" She said, finally.

"Yeah?"

"Just checking… Did we unleash some kind of violent demon and leave it lingering in my brother's bedroom?"

"Uh… I think so. Yeah."

"Hmm." Then, to inject a little levity—Kate's signature move: "This might be a tough one to explain to my parents."

"Ha. Yeah."

After the shock had passed and the caffeine had kicked in, we formulated a plan. We would go back to her brother's room, say the Lord's Prayer three times (I figured, one for each part of the Holy Trinity), and tell the demon to go away and never come back. We would reason with it and ask it to please remove itself from Kate's brother's room.

By the time we returned to Kate's house, her parents and brother had returned home. We checked her brother's bedroom, and the dark figure was gone. Kate's mother, after hearing our story, was unimpressed. Like my parents, she was simply a nonbeliever in anything supernatural (also, like my parents, she sent Kate to the shrink twice that week). However, she agreed to let us do our ritual.

"Just be quick about it," she sighed. "Your brother needs to go to bed."

After saying the prayers, we both instantly felt better. However, just to be on the safe side, we decided to sleep in the living room, instead of in Kate's room to further distance ourselves from the demon.

Kate went to gather some extra pillows and a pitcher of water, and I was left alone in the living room to set up our sleeping bags. Kate's parents, after seeing that the heat was not planning on relenting anytime soon, had decided to finally close all the windows and turn on the air conditioner. The relief it provided served to put me further at ease. I did my best psychic from Poltergeist impression to the empty room: "This house is clean." Sparky entered the room and seemed to be relaxed and happy. He licked my outstretched hand and then walked to the windows.

As I wrestled with Kate's unwieldy polyester sleeping bags, I heard two distinct sounds: Sparky barking and then the THUNK of multiple windows unlocking at once. I looked up. The windows—four of them—all opened slowly, their cranks turning eerily in unison.

I think I peed my pants a little. Once again, Sparky hightailed it from the room. *Some guard dog,* I thought to myself.

Kate's dad entered the room a moment later. "Why the hell are the windows open? Don't you know the air is on?"

"Uh…"

He closed and locked the windows and disappeared into the hallway, shoving past Kate and causing her to spill some of the water she was carrying.

"Jeez, what's his problem? Here are some pillows… What's wrong?"

In that moment, I decided to do something that I rarely did: keep my mouth shut. The Ouija Board had been my idea, and I felt a sudden pang of guilt for whatever fresh Hell it had wrought. I knew that I could return to the comfort of my own house and she would be stuck with God-knows-what lurking in her house (*oh, right,* I reminded myself, *apparently GOD ISN'T HERE.*) So I decided not to tell her about the windows. I did, however, suggest that we repeat the ritual in all remaining rooms of the house. You know, purely as a precaution.

Over the next few weeks, the strange activity

continued in Kate's house. One night she heard a low, faint growl coming from her brother's room that could not be attributed to Sparky. Lights flickered constantly, sending her father to the utility box several times or balancing precariously on ladders to tighten bulbs. Kate noticed hot spots— places where the temperature would be blistering for a brief moment. This was odd, as typically cold spots are associated with ghosts and spirits moving through a space. However, as we knew already, this was an entirely different kind of entity.

The worst interaction, however, came one night when Kate and her mother were cuddled up on the couch watching a video from Blockbuster. Kate's mother pressed the pause button on the remote to get some more water (hydration was clearly important to this family), and the VCR flew from its spot on top of the TV, hit the adjacent wall, and fell to the ground. A wisp of smoke slithered upward from the mouth flap that held the videocassette.

After a shocked silence, Kate's mother retreated to her bedroom and left a voicemail for her electrician. Kate gathered up the broken VCR and carried it to the large trashcans in the garage. As she entered the pitch-black garage, she heard the rumble of a deep, ominous laugh.

Kate would move out a little over a year after that night to start college. And while she would report the occasional strange occurrence—the usual flickering lights and hot spots—there were no other sightings of the shadow figure and no more flying appliances.

Shortly after Kate moved out the rest of her family would follow suit—though it was because her parents finally decided to divorce. As their marriage had been filled with its own variety of darkness, once they had separated there was nowhere for the darkness to reside. My parents had a different kind of darkness in their marriage, and it would take them another ten years, but eventually, they divorced too.

I guess I like to think that we brought an entity to the surface and drove it into the light somehow. After moving out of the house, Kate never saw the demon—or another ghost—again. She, and the rest of her family, went about their business and forged newer, happier paths for themselves. Sometimes I imagine that the demon got bored once it had no negative energy to sustain it. And so it pulled up stakes and drifted away to find someone else to terrorize. Or maybe good ultimately triumphed over evil, and the demon saw the error of its ways and changed – learning and evolving as we all hope to do as we move through life (or the afterlife, as the case may be). Or maybe that's just what I tell myself as a way of trying to justify my own less-than-stellar judgment at playing a game, and opening a door, that I shouldn't have.

I will never play with a Ouija Board again.

Author's Note

When I first started writing this collection, the political climate at the time made it feel like a rather strange and scary time to be a woman. It felt like a "dark night of the woman's soul," and I drew upon my own feelings and fears when crafting the narratives in this book. It was therefore important to me that all of the main characters in these stories were women, as each of the stories is meant to delve into the secret lives and inner worlds of women.

As you may have noticed, the main characters also share similar socioeconomic backgrounds—namely, upper-middle class. I made a deliberate choice here for two reasons: one, it is a perspective with which I am quite familiar, as I come from a similar background to that of my characters. It felt important for me, in keeping with this idea of expressing a sense of inner conflict and illustrating the struggles with which these characters are grappling, that I did not speak from a perspective that I did not fully understand. And two, entitlement is a bit of a theme in some of these stories, and in my own experience, I have found that often (though certainly not always!) entitlement goes hand in hand with higher socioeconomic status. This is not to say that women should be afraid of or discouraged from breaking the rules. It is just to say that unfortunately, society and apparently, the supernatural do not always tend to reward this kind of behavior.

I wanted to offer this context, not so that you will judge or dismiss my lovely characters (though they are flawed and not always the best decision-makers), but so that you will understand my choices as an author.

Appendix: Ghost Game Instructions

Dear Reader,

Do not play any of these games. I know that you might be curious, and that including these instructions may be tempting. After all, we as humans have an innate fascination with that which we do not understand. This fascination certainly extends to the paranormal. We think to ourselves, if I can just reach out and touch the other side, or see a ghost, or have unequivocal proof that the afterlife exists, perhaps my own mortality will not seem as terrifying. Perhaps my toiling through the mundane, or my suffering, or even my joy will have meant more than just temporary feelings contained within an even more temporary meat suitcase that carried my soul through the world.

I understand these thoughts and feelings. And I understand the temptation to want to play with and explore the paranormal. *After all,* you may say to yourself, *it's only a game.* By now you have read about my experience with the Ouija Board and the declaration that I made at the end of that story is entirely true: ever since that day several decades ago, I have not played with another Ouija Board. Nor do I intend to ever again. Similarly, I have not played any of these ghost games. Nor do I intend to. I recommend that you, Dear Reader, do not play them either.

Why, then, am I including the instructions? The

answer is simple: reading the instructions will add depth and color to the stories in this book. If you have access to the instructions, you can see where my protagonists bent the rules and things went off course. You can understand how the game is supposed to go, and how things went wrong. Some of these games—such as The Three Kings Game— are more complex than I described in the story, which was a narrative choice on my end. I also took some liberties with the closet game, as you will see in the instructions. It is simply my wish that you, Dear Reader, have a complete picture of the ghost games in order to enhance your reading experience.

If you do decide to try the games in a quest to amuse yourself (or answer nagging questions about life, death, and spirituality), you play at your peril. I hereby absolve myself of any responsibility for the consequences—good or bad—that may result. After all, you have been warned.

Yours in Terror,
Brooke MacKenzie

The Elevator Game

This game was first published on a Korean website. Play at your peril.

Minimum Number of Players: One

Materials: An empty elevator in a building with a minimum of ten floors

How to Play: The sequence of floors to visit during the elevator game are as follows: Enter from the first (or ground) floor. Then, travel to the fourth, second, tenth, fifth, and finally back to the first floor (which will hopefully take you to the tenth floor if you have performed the game correctly). However, pay close attention to what happens on the fifth floor, and whether or not the elevator descends to the first floor when you press the button.

1.) Enter the elevator from the first floor by yourself. Do not proceed with the game if anyone enters the elevator with you. You must be alone.

2.) Press the button for the fourth floor. Stay in the elevator when the doors open.

3.) Press the button for the second floor. Stay in the elevator when the doors open.

4.) Press the button for the sixth floor. Stay in the elevator when the doors open.

5.) Press the button for the second floor. Some have reported hearing a voice calling to them on the second floor during this middle section of the game. DO NOT REPLY. Stay in the elevator when the doors open.

6.) Press the button for the tenth floor. Stay in the elevator when the doors open.

7.) Press the button for the fifth floor, and be on the lookout for The Woman. The Woman will enter the elevator on this floor and attempt to engage with you. DO NOT ACKNOWLEDGE HER. Keep your eyes on the floor or the elevator buttons. She will attempt to lure you into another dimension. Some players have even reported that she has followed them home after the game is complete.

8.) Finally, press the button to head to the first floor. **If instead of going towards the first floor you instead begin to ascend to the tenth, you have performed the game correctly.** However— and this is very important—if instead you descend to the first floor, then you have done something wrong. You must leave the elevator as soon as it reaches the first floor. If the woman is on the elevator, **remember not to acknowledge her**.

9.) If you reach the tenth floor, you can either stay on the elevator or exit it. However, you must finish the game on the same elevator, so be sure to make note of the correct elevator if you do decide to leave it. Some have reported that upon attempting to leave the elevator, the woman will try one last time to engage with you. She may shriek as you cross the door's threshold. Keep your wits about you. Do not look at or engage with her.

10.) There are a few telltale signs that you have made it to the other dimension: the building will be dark and you will see a glowing red cross.

Finishing the Game:

*Alternatively, if you **do not** exit on the 10th floor:*

1.) Press the button for the first floor and keep pressing it until the elevator begins to move.

2.) Once you have reached the first floor, exit immediately. Do not exit on any other floors but the first. Do not acknowledge the woman if she is on the elevator. If anyone else gets on then do not speak to them either. Remain silent.

*If you **do** exit the elevator at the tenth floor:*

1.) When you get back to the SAME elevator, press the buttons in the same order you did in steps two through eight. This should take you to the fifth floor.

2.) Once you have reached the fifth floor, press the button for the first floor. Do not be surprised when you instead begin to ascend again to the tenth floor. Do not panic. You can press the button of any floor lower than ten to stop ascending, but you have to do it **before** you reach the tenth floor, no matter what.

3.) Once you have canceled the ascension and reached the first floor, make sure that everything seems normal to you. Check in with your senses: if anything smells, appears, sounds, or feels strange, do not exit the elevator. You must repeat step two until everything on the first floor seems normal.

4.) If all is as it should be, you may exit the elevator.

Important Information:

• Electronics often do not work in the other dimension.

• You *may* become disoriented and dizzy if you exit on the tenth floor. Pay attention to your feelings.

• If you get on the wrong elevator on your return trip then **do not enter the return sequence**. It will not work.

• Once again, if The Woman enters the elevator, DO NOT speak to her or look at her. This is one of the most important rules.

The Three Kings Game

In this game, a player uses mirrors to summon spirits from The Shadowside (another world). Play at your peril.

Minimum Number of Players: Two (one person to play the game and one "backup" person)

Materials:

- A large, empty room where no light can enter
- Candles and a lighter
- A bucket of water
- A mug
- A fan
- Two large mirrors (free standing)
- Three chairs
- An alarm clock (the one on your phone will suffice…make sure it is charged)
- A "power object": toy or meaningful item from your childhood

How to Play:

1.) First and foremost, brief your "backup" person on his or her role, and make sure that he or she is physically present for the entirety of the ritual.

2.) Start setting up at 11 p.m. sharp. Place one chair in the center of the room, facing north. This will be your "throne." Place the other two chairs to the left and right, at a minimum of arm's length, facing your throne. These will serve as the "fool" and "queen" chairs.

3.) Place the two large mirrors on the queen and fool chairs, facing you and each other. They should stand at a 90-degree angle. If you sit on the throne and face straight ahead (north), you should be able to see your own reflection in each of the two mirrors without having to turn your head.

4.) Place the bucket of water and the mug in front of you, just out of reach.

5.) Place the fan behind you and turn it to low power. Leave it on until the game concludes.

6.) Once you have finished setting up, turn off the lights, leave the door to the room where you intend to play the game open, and go to your bedroom.

7.) Put your candle, lighter, alarm clock, and power object by your bed. Set your alarm for 3:30 a.m.. Try to get some rest.

8.) When your alarm goes off at 3:30 a.m., do not turn on the light. you will have exactly three minutes to grab your phone, sit in your throne, and light your candle. **You must be seated no later than 3:33 a.m., and you must be holding your power object.** Your backup person should be in a different room, and have his or her phone ready to go.

Important Information: You and your backup person MUST abort the game, leave your apartment, and not return until **6:00 a.m. at the latest** if any of the following have happened:
- Your alarm did not go off
- You are not seated by 3:33 a.m.

• The fan has turned off (remember, you left it on)

• The door has closed (remember, you left it open)

If none of the above has happened, proceed with the game. Be sure your candle is lit as you sit in your throne.

• DO NOT look directly into either mirror
• DO NOT let the candle go out

9.) Stare straight ahead into the darkness. Let your mind wander. From your perspective, you are the king, and the other chairs are the queen and the fool. However, from the perspective of the other occupants of the chairs, THEY are king, and the other chairs (including yours) belong to the queen or the fool (therefore resulting in "three kings"). It is important to note that you could either be king, queen, or fool, depending on the perspective of the spirits.

10.) You will hear and see strange things. Whispering, shadows, or any number of terrifying phenomena. And still, you must keep staring straight ahead. DO NOT look at the mirrors.

11.) DO NOT let the candle go out. If anything strange happened to you during the game (for instance, if your body was moved), the fan should serve as backup number one and blow out the candle, thus ending the game and (hopefully) returning you to your senses.

12.) At 4:34 a.m. exactly, the game is over. Your backup person should call your name. If you do not respond, he or she should call your phone.

If that does not work, he or she should enter the room and, without making physical contact with you, throw the bucket and mug filled with water on you. At this point, any trance you might be in will be broken.

The Closet Game

Note: In the story, the instructions and desired result have some fictionalized elements. Below are the actual instructions for the game.

In this game, a single player summons a demon. Please note: demons are NOT to be trifled with. Never taunt or provoke a demon. Also, take CAUTION when lighting a match within an enclosed space. Before playing, please ensure that you have cleared out any flammable items and have adequate space for lighting a match safely. Play at your peril.

Minimum Number of Players: One

Materials: Matches and a walk-in closet with no windows

How to Play:

1.) Locate a walk-in closet with enough space for you to enclose yourself and safely light a match. The light should be off, and there should be no external light whatsoever.

2.) Face the closet door, shut it, and stand in the darkness for a minimum of two minutes. Remain silent. Stay as still as possible.

3.) Hold a match in front of you and say, "Show me the light or leave me in darkness."

4.) Listen carefully. If you hear a whisper, quickly light the match. You MUST light the match on your first try, or else a demon may grab you and drag you into eternal darkness. If you do not hear anything, DO NOT turn around. Wait until you hear the whispers.

5.) Keep the match lit while you're in the closet. Slowly open the door and step outside.

6.) Close the closet door behind you. You will have summoned a demon. Whenever you look in the closet with the lights off, you will see two glowing red eyes staring back at you.

Bloody Mary

This popular slumber party game is rooted in legend, which has several different versions. Some believe that her origins are historical in nature, and that she is the spirit of Mary I, Queen of England. She had a penchant for slaughtering Protestants (she herself was a Catholic), which earned her the nickname "Bloody Mary." Another version of the legend centers around Mary Worth – a witch who lived in Chicago around the time of the Civil War. She was a practitioner of the dark arts, and eventually burned at the stake. A more modern interpretation is that Mary is a woman whose face was badly mutilated in a car accident, and when she is summoned, she will reach out of the mirror and scratch the players' faces – mutilating *them* in turn. Play at your peril.

Minimum Number of Players: One

Materials: Dark room with a mirror (usually the bathroom works best), one lit candle

How to Play:

1.) Turn of the lights in the bathroom and light a candle

2.) Face the mirror

3.) Say, "Bloody Mary" three times. If you are playing with more than one player, it is usually most effective to have one volunteer summon her. If she appears in the mirror, she may try to reach out and scratch your face, or even attempt to trap you in the mirror. She has also been known to drive players mad.

Variations:

- Cross your arms over your chest while saying, "Bloody Mary"
- Say, "Bloody Mary" a dozen or more times
- Say, "I believe in Mary Worth" instead of "Bloody Mary"

The Answer Man

Note: In the book this game was referred to as "The Telephone Game". It originated in Japan. Play at your peril.

Minimum Number of Players: Ten

Materials: Each player must have a cell phone (ideally a "burner phone," as the phones should be destroyed once the game ends)

How to Play:

1.) Gather ten participants in a circle. Each person should have the phone number of the person to his or her immediate left.

2.) On the count of three, each participant calls the person on the left. The result should be a busy signal or the call will be sent to voicemail. However, for one person, the call will be answered by The Answer Man.

3.) If he answers, the player may ask The Answer Man a question.

4.) The Answer Man will then ask the player a question in turn. The participant MUST answer this question correctly or suffer the consequences.

5.) When the call is over, the participant must tell The Answer Man that he or she must go. When The Answer Man says goodbye, the player must hang up.

6.) When the call has been successfully terminated, all players must destroy their phones.

Important Information:

- DO NOT hang up on The Answer Man before saying goodbye.

- DO NOT attempt to pass the phone to other players or put The Answer Man on speakerphone. He chooses one player, and one player only.

- The player typically gets to ask ONE question. If the Answer Man attempts to keep the player on the line, he or she must insist on saying goodbye. DO NOT allow The Answer Man to stay on the line.

The Bathtub Game

This game originated in Japan. Play at your peril.

Minimum Number of Players: One

Materials: A full bathtub (a shower will not suffice), and towels or a bathmat to avoid slipping

How to Play:

1.) Play this game at night. Fill the bathtub with water, submerge yourself, and turn off the lights. You should be facing the tap.

2.) While in the tub, wash your hair while repeating, "Daruma-san fell down," over and over again.

3.) You will experience a vision. Just relax and watch it unfold. A black-haired Japanese woman in a white nightgown will be standing in a bathtub, for reasons not known to you or anyone. She will fall and land face first onto the tap. It punctures her eye and ultimately kills her.

4.) Ask her aloud, "Why did you fall in the tub?" It is not clear whether or not she slipped or was pushed.

5.) Once the vision has concluded, you will have summoned her spirit. Keep your eyes closed. Climb out of the tub slowly and carefully. Exit the bathroom and close the door behind you. Then, and only then, it is safe to open your eyes.

6.) Crawl into bed and go to sleep. The game will begin the next morning when you wake up.

7.) You will see her over your shoulder when you look in a mirror, or in your peripheral vision as you go throughout your day. Her clothing is tattered, her black hair is tangled, and her skin is rotting after too much time in the tub. She will only have one eye. But she will stare at you relentlessly.

8.) As the day goes on she will get closer and closer to you. Feel free to yell, "Tomare!" Which means, "Stop!" And then quickly run away. This will, in theory, allow you to have some space from her.

Important Information:

• No matter what, do not allow her to catch you. Ever.

• To end the game, throw your glance over your right shoulder and look at her (you may not want to, but you must). Shout, "Kitta!", which means, "I cut you loose." Swing your arm down in a chopping motion. If you have done this correctly, the game will be over.

• If you have NOT done this correctly, well......run and hide.

The Hide-and-Seek Game

This game originated in Japan. Play at your peril.

Minimum Number of Players: One

Materials:

- One stuffed doll with limbs
- Rice, enough to stuff the doll full
- One needle
- One crimson thread
- One pair of nail clippers
- One knife
- One cup of salt water
- A bathtub filled with water
- A hiding place purified by incense and ofuda. There must be a TV in there.

How to Play:

1.) Cut the doll open, remove its stuffing, and re-stuff it with rice. This will attract spirits.

2.) Using the nail clippers, cut a few of your nails and put the clippings inside of the doll with the rice. This will bind you to the doll.

3.) Sew up the opening with the crimson thread. When you finish sewing, instead of cutting the thread, take the remainder and tie it around the doll.

4.) Fill your bathtub with water.

5.) Go to your hiding place and put the cup of saltwater in it.

6.) Give a name to your doll. The name can be any but your own.

7.) At 3:00 a.m., say, "[Your Name] is the first it," to the doll three times.

8.) Go to the bathroom and put the doll into the water-filled tub.

9.) Turn off all of the lights in your house, go back to the hiding place, and switch on the TV. This will act as a safeguard against any unwanted spirits that may enter your home during the game.

10.) After counting to ten with your eyes closed, return to the bathroom with the knife in your hand. The doll will still be floating in the bathtub.

11.) Say to the doll, "I have found you, [Doll's Name]." Stab the doll with the knife and cut the crimson thread binding it.

12.) Say, "You are the next it, [Doll's Name]." Return the doll to the bathtub.

13.) Run back to the hiding place and hide. The doll will come looking for you.

14.) Pour half of the cup of salt water into your mouth. Do not swallow it.

15.) Emerge from you hiding place and start looking for the doll. Note: The doll will not necessarily be where you left it. Keep the salt water in your mouth.

16.) When you find the doll, pour the salt water in the cup over it. Then, spit out the salt water onto it.

17.) Say, "I win!" three times. This will end the game. Allow the doll to dry, burn it, and discard its remains.

Important Information:

• Do not leave your hiding place without the saltwater.

- Do not stop the game until you have played it to completion.

Ouija Board

It may look like a simple board game, but it is quite dangerous. Play at your peril.

Minimum Number of Players: Two

Materials: Ouija Board and planchette. It is best to play in a darkened room.

How to Play:

1.) The players should sit facing each other with their knees touching. The Ouija Board should be placed on their knees.

2.) Both players should place their fingers lightly on the planchette. To warm it up, purposely move it in a circle around the board.

3.) Begin asking questions. It is best to start with simple "yes" or "no" questions. It may take a moment for the planchette to move. Be patient.

4.) When you are finished playing, say goodbye to the spirits and slide the planchette over the "GOODBYE" at the bottom of the board and then remove your hands. This is an important step.

Important Information:

• Do not believe everything the board tells you. Often the spirit to whom you are speaking is not necessarily who it says it is.

• Do not ask for physical signs of the spirit's presence.

• Always say goodbye and close the board when you are finished.

Acknowledgements

First and foremost, I would like to thank the wonderful team at Gravestone Press—in particular, Stuart Holland and Dorothy Davies—for believing in this book and treating it with such tender loving care. Your kindness and professionalism have been invaluable to me.

Endless gratitude goes to Mayumi Shimose Poe, my beta reader and first editor, whose feedback was invaluable to making this book what it is. I would also like to thank Larina Alton for providing excellent legal advice and expertise. To Louise Crawford, my literary publicist, I thank you for joining me on this exciting journey. I would like to thank Ed Velandria (www.velandria.com) for the amazing cover and website design, and Leanna Flecky (www.leannajeanphoto.com) for making me look beautiful in the author photo when I was not even three months postpartum.

Several friends were the source of important inspiration and guidance for this book as well. My thanks and love go out to Jessica, Clare, Elyssa, Rebecca, Kelly, Kelly, Monica, Kari, Rachel, Kellyn, and Dulcea. I thank you for your generosity of spirit. I would also like to thank Colette for encouraging me to keep going when the rejections were getting to me. You were right, and it was worth it.

There are many locations throughout New York City that served as favorite writing spots while working on this book. I would particularly like to thank the women-only co-working space, Luminary (www.luminary-nyc.com), Café Wattle in Kips Bay, and The Crooked Knife on 14th Street. I am lucky to serve as Board Chair of an incredible nonprofit, New York Writers Coalition (www.nywriterscoalition.org), and feel grateful to be surrounded and supported by Board Members who are truly passionate about both community and writing.

Finally, and most importantly, I would like to thank my family. My parents, Janet and David; my sister Molly; my brother-in-law Ty; my nieces, Lily and Chase. Chase, in particular, has rooted for this book since day one, and has been a steadfast reader and editor of each of the stories. We are truly kindred spirits in our love of horror, and it is for this reason that the book is dedicated to her. If she should so choose, I think she would make a great writer one day. I also want to thank my Aunties: Reenie and Dana for teaching me about strength, grace, and unconditional love. I would also like to thank my beloved Aunt Phoebe, who passed away in 2021, for always telling me that I should pursue my dreams of becoming a writer, and for always being a willing audience for my poems and stories. My Uncle Eric indulged the horror lover in me during my younger years, and my Aunt Geri-Anne has shared my work with many others, and for that, I thank them. I would like to thank the MacKenzie/Applegate side of the family: Stephen, Lauren, Mark, Nancy, and Monroe. A special shout out goes to Helen, who consistently reads everything I write. I honor the memory of Elizabeth MacKenzie, and thank her for building such an incredible family that I am so grateful to have joined.

To my husband, Sean, and my daughter, Maeve, you both inspire and motivate me every day. Sean, thank you for fully encouraging me to create space in my life for writing. You are the best cheerleader, and your belief in me has carried me through on many occasions. This book would not have happened if it were not for you and your unwavering support. Maeve, the world is a more magical and blissful place because you are in it. I love you both more than I can express.

Cover Design: Ed Velandria
(www.velandria.com)
Author Photo: Leanna Flecky
(www.leannajeanphoto.com)